Keeping in Touch

Keeping in Touch

Anjali Joseph

SCRIBE
Melbourne · London

Scribe Publications
2 John St, Clerkenwell, London, WC1N 2ES, United Kingdom
18–20 Edward St, Brunswick, Victoria 3056, Australia
3754 Pleasant Ave, Suite 100, Minneapolis, Minnesota 55409, USA

First published by Context, an imprint of Westland Publications
Private Limited, in 2021
Published by Scribe 2022

Internal pages designed by by SÜRYA, New Delhi

Printed and bound in the UK by CPI Group (UK) Ltd,
Croydon CR0 4YY

Scribe is committed to the sustainable use of natural resources and
the use of paper products made responsibly from those resources.

978 1 957363 00 4 (US edition)
978 1 913348 66 3 (UK edition)
978 1 922310 62 0 (Australian edition)
978 1 922586 29 2 (ebook)

Catalogue records for this book are available from
the British Library and the National Library of Australia.

scribepublications.com
scribepublications.co.uk
scribepublications.com.au

To Simon, with love

Contents

1

Everlasting Lucifer

VED VED SAT in the executive lounge at Heathrow and sipped his peppermint tea. With a sigh, a slender woman appeared next to him. She put her satchel on the bar and followed it with a canvas bag, a book, four magazines, a glass of champagne, and a plate holding girl-sized amounts of salmon, salad, cheese, and chocolate pudding. She sat down, sighed again, crossed her legs and took off her hat to shake out long black hair. What was she wearing—some sort of jumpsuit? She smiled at the huge window, beyond which, in the darkness, planes were taxiing, landing or allowing passengers to embark.

No, said Ved Ved to himself. He was thirty-seven. He'd had enough of executive lounge hipsters, trust fund kids, with their rising inflections and their perfect skin. Don't look, he thought.

She lifted thin arms to coil her hair, and speared it with what appeared to be a single blue chopstick. Ved saw some armpit fuzz, and wasn't put off. He felt a pain in his navel. He stared at her cheekbone, and one long, slightly upward-slanting eye. She looked round, smiled at him amicably, and sipped her drink.

She wasn't going to talk to him. He had just begun to contemplate this when he heard some idiot blurt, 'Where are you travelling to?'

It was him. She looked up, glass in hand.

'Where are you going?' he said, and smiled.

She was looking at him. He wanted to die.

'Bombay,' she said. Her voice was clear and light.

'Oh, so am I,' he said. 'Nine o'clock?'

She nodded.

'Are you studying? Is that where you live? Bombay, Mumbai,' he went on.

She remained calm and open.

'Do you live in Mumbai?' he continued.

'No. I'm going back to Assam. But I'm breaking the journey to spend a couple of days with friends.'

'You live in Assam? I'm sorry,' he stopped himself. 'I'm interrupting your quiet time. My name's Ved.' He pulled himself together and put out his hand, went back to the usual approach, boyish, friendly, etc.

'Keteki,' she said, not taking the hand but smiling, less from pleasure, he noticed, than as a gesture, a glass of cool water offered to a guest.

'That's a beautiful name,' Ved said. 'What does it mean?'

'It's the name of a bird,' she said.

Ved looked at her full mouth. 'It must be a beautiful bird.'

'It's nothing much to look at. But it's a trickster.'

'A what?'

'A trickster. It leaves its babies in other birds' nests, and it looks and tries to sound like a bird of prey so other birds leave it alone.'

'Oh,' Ved said.

A few white hairs did decorative things near her ear. Her eyeliner had made a blob at the outer corner of her eye. He had never realised how appealing these things were: armpit fuzz, smudged eyeliner, white hairs. Secretly, for years, he must have been infatuated with them all.

'But the keteki bird has a sweet voice.' She smiled. 'Excuse me. I just want to go and ... before we board.'

'Oh! That won't be for a ... Do you want me to keep an eye on your stuff?'

'Sweet of you.' She smiled at him and, glowing, he guarded her plate, bags, magazines and champagne flute.

'Oh, look,' said Keteki. 'They've written your name twice.'

Ved Ved, said the piece of paper the driver was holding. Ved wiped his face. 'Er, no,' he said. 'That's my name.'

'They're not actually the same name,' he said when they were in the car. 'Can you turn on the air conditioning, please? Excuse me?'

In better Hindi, she asked the driver to start the air conditioning. He laughed and said it was on. They swung under a flyover.

'But they're spelt the same,' Keteki said.

'One means a doctor,' Ved said. 'The other means knowledge. I guess it's an old-fashioned transliteration.'

'Isn't it the same etymology?' she asked. 'Knowledge knowledge. Clever-clever, like you say in England.'

In his suite at eleven in the morning, Ved sipped a gin and tonic, and looked across the Arabian Sea, which was dirty. So was he. Very soon, he'd do something about that. The bathroom here was nice. He would avail of it, as Indians said, in no time at all. He wished he could avail of Keteki. A remark she'd made in the car as he was dropping her off at her friend's house, somewhere after the Sealink, had stayed with him.

'Venture capital,' she said. 'Okay. So you're going to meet this man who wants to reboot his light bulb company. With the bulb that lasts a long time. Good name, by the way. But, Ved, what do you do for joy?'

'For—?' said Ved.

'Joy,' she repeated in that clear voice. Long fingers pushed back her hair. Now the air conditioning was definitely on. Ved could smell himself, and he'd smelled better.

'You mean fun?' he said.

'No. Joy. What makes you feel joyful, like a child?'

He looked into her eyes, a lighter brown than his, a trace of eyeliner under them like smoke.

'Um,' he said.

In the last few years, Ved had given up on having girlfriends. Instead, he'd have sex with women and behave slightly dismissively before he left or got them to leave. A callous remark, a joke, an inability to remember things they'd said in conversation. He wasn't sure why he was doing it, and when he noticed, he'd compensate by being extra nice before he fled.

In an odd way, the more he liked the girl, whoever she was, the more he felt relieved after things ended, almost more than after sex. He'd feel unburdened, take a long shower, and wander round his flat in soft cotton clothes.

At four-thirty he went downstairs, feeling calm and cool. He had on a clean suit, a new shirt.

Ganesh Appaiah was in the Sea Lounge.

'Ved,' he said, shaking Ganesh's hand. He noticed how still the other man was.

'Good to meet you, Ved,' said Ganesh.

'What shall we drink?' Ved asked.

'Maybe some tea?'

Ganesh had a table with a sea view. They ordered tea. Ved felt more relaxed than in a long time. Usually, he drank coffee and talked fast. Here he was though, drinking tea, in an air-conditioned room with waiters in white uniforms and red turbans, looking out at the soothingly brown sea.

'I like it here,' Ved said.

Ganesh smiled. Everyone, Ved noticed, was treating him as though he was a child. And he didn't mind.

'My parents are from India, originally,' Ved said.

Ganesh nodded.

Tea, thought Ved, sipping his cup of Assam. It smelled fragrant, of fermentation, sweat, armpits, reality. He reminded himself to stay in control. 'I've had a look at the documentation,' he said. 'The product looks very interesting. It's not exactly a CFL, it's not an incandescent, it's not an LED. How are you categorising it?' Ved became distracted by a shortcakey biscuit, and ate it. He heard Keteki's clear voice: 'Filament is a lovely word.'

'We haven't come up with a generic name yet,' Ganesh said. 'You have the information pack, and our engineer will explain further when you visit the plant. But we're calling it an intelligent filament. It learns to shine and hold its radiance the more it's used. And we're reviving the Lucifer brand. This bulb is called the Everlasting Lucifer, as you know.'

Ved laughed. 'Yes, about that. I wonder if it's going to be a problem. The connotations…'

'Well,' said Ganesh. 'My grandfather effectively ran the firm when it was still British-owned, and he told me that originally Lucifer meant the morning star, the bringer of light. And I believe that, in the Bible, Lucifer is a Latin word also used for Jesus. Have you seen the old advertisements, by the way?'

'Yes.' Ved opened the folder to colour reproductions: a cute devil assisting a small child to study in the evening. *Lucifer brand: let there be light.* 'What about everlasting though? Why would a company that makes light bulbs want to make one that lasts forever?'

'Everlasting is perhaps poetic licence, Ved,' said Ganesh. 'The bulb should last about forty or fifty years. That's four times as long as an LED. And so we expect it in time to become the recommended bulb for use in all sorts of institutions as well as homes. There is a lot of potential, here and abroad. As you know, the price of CFLs and LEDs is subsidised by the government, so ultimately there is no reason why that couldn't happen with this bulb. But at this point of course we haven't been able to do actual trials of its durability. We're hoping to roll it out to try in homes at a reduced initial price.'

Ved nodded. 'Well, I'm looking forward to meeting the development team tomorrow,' he said.

'I wanted to invite you home,' Ganesh said. 'But my wife's out, and I wasn't sure if you'd be tired since you only arrived this morning. Would you like to go out to dinner?'

Ved waved a hand. 'Don't worry. I'm supposed to meet someone this evening.'

In the lift, Ved wondered if part of the reason he'd been pleased about this trip was that he could visit Rupal Madam again. As he aged, he noticed himself becoming more brutal but also more sentimental; he felt the urge to revisit places and experiences that, if only in imagined memories, seemed to represent past satisfactions. He missed his childhood, or thought he did: the feeling of being a child, being loved, indulged, safe, a feeling he rarely remembered having when actually a child, still pulled him. In India, a place he'd spent a few early years, the feeling became general: here, people were in and out of their childhood, no matter their age.

Anyway, it was silly not to do more work here. Growth was still good, and the new Hindu nationalist government seemed focused on encouraging investment.

The process of getting a date with Rupal Madam had been streamlined. He'd called the old number when he agreed to the trip, and had been told to email her office instead. An assistant sent him an order number, a list of preferences and a secure payment form.

Adding the title 'luxury consultant' to her name and address was a nice touch. Presumably this was so that, even if one's secretary made the booking, there was no awkwardness.

'You're … mnemogenic,' he'd said to Keteki before she got out of the car the previous night. 'I really hope we see each other again.'

She nodded. 'You've read your Nabokov, huh.'

Now, as the lift approached the seventeenth floor of Rupal Madam's building on Nepean Sea Road, Ved felt himself getting half a hard-on.

The flat had been redecorated. It was light and airy, not unlike his hotel suite. The sofa was upholstered in raw silk; a large golden Buddha sat against one wall.

'So you're back, beta?'

At the sound of Rupal Madam, Ved's hard-on left the building. Her voice was grating, her accent slightly off when she spoke English. He turned. Her eyes flashed anger. 'I never thought I'd see someone from this family in service, in a job, working for other people. You think the world owes you a living. When your father gets home, he will speak to you.'

Ved laughed.

'Something is funny?'

He looked at her. She was dressed in a sari and cardigan, and held a large wooden paddle hairbrush, as specified on his preferences form. 'I'm sorry,' said Ved, unusually politely. 'I think I've made a mistake. You know how people say you can never go home again?'

Ved had phoned Keteki five times. It was not cool behaviour. On his third day in Mumbai, she sent him a WhatsApp message. 'Sorry Ved!! I've been catching up with old friends. Have you got time for a bite this evening? Would be great to see you!'

He was meditating, using the app on his phone. Ved saw the message and told himself to focus. A minute later she called, and he snatched at the phone, dropped it, picked it up, and yelped, 'Hi? Hello? Keteki?'

For a second or two there was silence, as when, in the past, a trunk call was connected. '*Ved*,' she said.

'Yes,' he said, instantly and wholly present.

'Ved, I have a *favour* to ask. I was supposed to stay with another friend this evening, but she's had to go out of town, so I'm free. I thought maybe we could have dinner together and, if it's not inconvenient, I could crash in your hotel room? I've got an early flight tomorrow, so I won't be in your way for long.' Her voice was light as ever, but higher, vibrating more.

Ved said, 'It's kind of beautiful, isn't it?'

Above them, the bulb shone in the socket. Ved stood back from the standard lamp. The more Keteki gazed at the Lucifer, the brighter it seemed to become, though its glow remained soft and pure.

'*Oh*,' she said. 'Yes.'

'It's like the light from an incandescent,' Ved said.

'Yes, it doesn't distort colour,' she said. 'But … oh. Oh, I see.'

'What?' Ved said, touching her elbow. Her face brightened, but she didn't answer.

They left the bulb in the lamp and Keteki's three small bags on a marble inlay table in his room, and went out to dinner.

As they sat down in the dimly lit, slightly colonial surroundings, all wooden shutters and a fan gently whirring, Ved smiled. 'You look really beautiful. I love that dress. It's simple, but so elegant.'

'First of all,' he said. 'What brought you to Heathrow and to the lounge?'

'Oh, I—'

'Could I have the wine list, please?' Ved asked the waiter. 'This one? Great, we'll have a bottle? Is that fine for you?'

'What a treat,' Keteki said. 'I love this place. How did you get a reservation at such short notice? The hotel, I guess.'

'So, you were going to tell—oh yes. I will try it. Mm, that's nice. Thanks.' He waited till their glasses had been filled and took a larger sip. 'You were going to tell me what took you to England.'

'Scotland, actually. I was helping a friend curate an exhibition. That's one of the various things I do freelance.' She put down her glass. 'Fifteen years, and I still find it difficult to explain what I do in a sentence.' She shrugged.

'But how old are you?' Ved asked. 'When we met I thought—'

'Thirty-nine.'

'Oh really? I'm thirty-eight.'

She leaned forward and looked him dead in the eye. 'That must be why I feel so connected to you. Do you think we were twins in another life?'

'Ha ha. Er, I hope not,' said Ved. He felt the back of his neck. 'What was the exhibition you were working on? Where was it, Edinburgh?'

'Glasgow. Domestic artefacts and interior decoration from the Arts and Crafts era. My favourite thing in it was a milk jug.'

'A milk jug?' Ved smiled. He'd decided what to order. 'What was it like?'

Keteki looked at him. 'Simple,' she said.

'This steak isn't bad,' Ved said a little later. 'Nor is the wine. Though I wonder if they stored it at the right temperature.'

He said, 'I don't know why, but something always happens to me when I'm in India. Smells do things to me. Like the smell of the rain.' It was falling now, a soft curtain muffling the sound of a car horn outside.

'I don't normally talk this much,' Ved said. 'I don't know what's going on. You're so— Normally, there's something, something that turns me off. But you—'

'Sweet of you, Ved.'

He laughed. 'I guess people say things like that to you a lot?'

Keteki smiled, the corners of her eyes crinkling almost secretively. 'People are so kind,' she murmured. 'Especially given that it's so hard to remember details. Names, that sort of thing. Although not yours—Ved Ved, there can't be too many of you in the telephone directory.'

As they walked back to the hotel along the seafront, he mused, 'In India, in the monsoon, it feels like nothing can ever really be clean. Do you know what I mean? The rain washes things, but there'll always be something. One of those tiny green leaves, or an insect.'

Back in his room, he said, 'Let's see what's in this mini bar. I feel like a brandy. Shall we have a brandy?'

'Ved,' said Keteki, 'I'm turning the main light off.'

They sat on the couch in the turret window, in the glamour of the single Everlasting Lucifer.

'The sea,' Ved said. 'It looks … more beautiful in the dark.'

Keteki's voice, remote, said, 'You can hear it slapping the wall when you walk on Strand Road.'

He reached for her. Not long after, in the dark, he was saying, 'Wow. Your nipples taste of cigarette smoke. Or tea, I don't know.'

Afterwards, Keteki slept. Ved didn't till near dawn. He kept feeling she was about to leave. And yet, she was sleeping peacefully. Of course she was going to leave. He must do something, make a plan to visit her.

'Ved,' she was saying. 'It's six-thirty. I'm making some tea.'

'No,' he said. 'Don't get up.' But she was already up. Her small bags were packed. She wore jeans and a cotton top. Her hair was tied up, no doubt fastened with a chopstick.

'Give me a minute,' he said. He went to the bathroom. When he came out, she was in front of the lamp, gingerly removing the Everlasting Lucifer.

'It's so lovely,' she said. 'When it's on, there almost seems to be something dancing inside.'

She put the bulb on a table. Ved came up to stroke her arm. Instead, she handed him a cup of tea.

'I'll come to see you,' he said. 'Or come to London. I'll send you a ticket.'

'I don't usually travel business class,' she said. 'I was upgraded.'

'When are we going to see each other again?' Ved said.

Keteki smiled. The daylight, after the glow of the Everlasting Lucifer, was oddly disappointing. 'Does the bulb really last forever?'

'No,' Ved said. 'We might have to think about the name. An incandescent lasts about a thousand hours. That's six months. An energy saving bulb lasts ten times as long, maybe five years. An LED could last fifteen years. The Everlasting should last forty or fifty years. You didn't answer the question. Let's set a date, even provisionally. I've never been to Assam.'

She sat crosslegged in the silk chair, holding her cup and saucer. 'You know, Ved,' she said, 'people *like* being lied to. And I'm good at it, I won't deny that. But,' and she stared at the standard lamp, melancholic, 'I'm getting a little tired of it.'

Ved Ved sat down on a loveseat. 'I'm sorry,' he said. 'You haven't even got home. You're in transit. We can talk about this in a few days. Or whenever.' He sipped the tea and smelled her on his fingers.

At Mumbai airport, so pleasantly redone and so appealingly lit, Ved had an attack of sadness and nostalgia, the fear of the end of the world, the sense that his stomach was falling out of his trunk, slowly, endlessly. He was a failure; he would never amount to anything. He wanted to talk to Keteki. Her phone was off. He wanted to tell her what he felt, but he didn't want to use words. He sent her a message on WhatsApp with the following emoticons: an Easter Island stone head, a sailing boat, comedy and tragedy masks, a postcard, an aeroplane in flight, seen from above, a building that might have been a church, with a pink heart above its door, a dark-haired girl with a star on her brow, a monkey hiding its mouth, two oriental matryoshka dolls side by side, a crystal ball, a red telephone set with push buttons and a syringe from the tip of which dripped two red drops.

Two days later, after he'd got home, paid the cleaner, opened his post, dealt with his email, gone back to work, written a report on the Everlasting Lucifer, and gone out with a girl he met on an app to a few different bars in St James's, where all the men were very closely shaven and dressed in bespoke Souster and Hicks, he was walking home at 3 a.m. when Keteki replied.

'Oh Ved,' said the message. 'Don't you think everlasting might just be a little too long?'

2

This year's goddess

'So,' Puwali pehi asked, 'what are your plans for the day?'

Keteki, sitting at the corner of the kitchen table, grinned. In the house in Guwahati where her father and Puwali pehi, his youngest sister, had grown up, this had been the children's table. Puwali pehi, who hadn't married, had kept the table and the L-shaped bench that went with it in her ground-floor apartment in the old house.

'You might as well ask what are my plans for my life,' Keteki said.

'Well?' said her aunt.

Keteki shrugged. 'Arts and Crafts at Home, over. Now, the next thing. Go through emails, reply to people I should have replied to months ago. Sit with Manek-da so he can prepare my tax return. Email other people to remind them I exist in case they want to use me in a future project. Post pictures online of things we did. Think about what I would like to achieve in this human birth.' She laughed at the last remark, and tried to stretch out her shoulders. Her body was still getting used to having arrived.

Puwali pehi sipped her tea. 'I'm so happy to see you,' she said. 'But lately, every time you come back to Guwahati, you seem to be having a personality crisis. Maybe you'd prefer to take up a normal job again.'

'Maybe,' Keteki said. She had a flashback of the industrial estate in northern Bombay where she'd sat drawing designs for horrible furnishing fabric in her first job seventeen years earlier. 'No, not that. I hated that. But, something, you're right, I have to change something. The way things are, going off, helping other people with things, making them happy for a while, then starting again, it's getting boring.' She considered. 'People like having me around.'

'Including me,' said her aunt. 'By the way, how is your Joy mama?'

Keteki smiled. 'I must phone him,' she said. 'I want to go to Jorhat soon and see him. Maybe after Puja is over.'

That evening, sitting on the bed in her room with her friend Pia, Keteki complained. 'What's a reasonable use of a life, anyway?'

Pia's eyes went round. 'What do you mean, Ketu ba?'

'Who decides?' Keteki said. 'What else should I be doing? Get married, have some children, worry about their schooling? Join my husband's business, start a business of my own ... open a shop. No, a bou*tique*.' She brooded. 'Join a ladies' business organisation. Refer to myself as a ontro-pron-*oor*.' She laughed. 'I can't decide whether to be annoyed with everyone else or just take nothing seriously.'

The room was dim, with only a table lamp on. Its red silk shade provided a warm glow and extravagant pools of shadow.

'But don't you ever want to get married, Ketu ba,' asked Pia. 'I mean, haven't you ever been in love?'

Keteki sighed. For a moment she considered explaining that since she had been four years old, she had trusted almost no one, that falling in love was, she had found, a dubious blessing, and that even if she did fall in love, she had no illusions it would clarify anything else in her life. On the contrary: she'd then have to deal with not only her own unwise decisions, but someone else's too.

But Pia had come to tell Keteki about her engagement to a man her parents had found, who had a good job managing a tea estate in upper Assam. There was no point in being a drag. 'I've fallen in love now and again,' Keteki said, and smiled apologetically. 'But nothing ever worked out somehow. Pia, should we have a toast? I seem to remember there was some good brandy somewhere.'

'A brandy? It's so late,' Pia began.

'Let me see,' Keteki said. She began to root in the bottom of her cupboard, removing one long leather boot at which she made a face, before replacing it. 'Here we are. Not champagne, but champagne cognac. There was a fellow from the French consulate in Delhi,' she explained. 'Jean-Luc? Jean-Pierre? Anyway. They get things in the diplomatic bag, you know.'

She left the room and returned with two tumblers. 'Not the right glass, but it'll have to do,' she said. 'Oh, it's still good.' The liquor was amber and smelled of caramel.

'Happy Puja, and congratulations,' she said.

'Aren't you even going to come for the anjali today?' Pehi asked the next morning.

'You look nice,' Keteki said. Her aunt was wearing a green-and-gold mekhela sador. 'No, you carry on, I think I'll go for a walk before things get crazy in the evening.' She made some coffee and wandered around the front room, near the window. Outside, there was the sound of drums and the scent of rain. She thought of the large idol of Durga at Barowari, looking at her devotees from slanted eyes.

Keteki took a bath and got dressed. The weather was cooler; it seemed to be the first day of autumn. As she walked in the drizzle of the morning, she heard car horns. By evening there would be long traffic jams and angry drivers. It was strange that Puja, supposedly about worship, should bring such chaos and aggression. What can you expect, she heard her uncle quipping, from a Bengali festival. But she also remembered the first time she and a cousin had visited the Kamakhya temple in Guwahati, a disorienting process of queueing, waiting, going inside the rock-cut building and down to the sanctum, where there was an opening in the rock and iron-reddened water—the goddess's menstrual blood—to drink. The place had an enormous, impersonal charge; it had felt like sticking your finger in the electrical socket on top of a volcano.

During Puja, people suddenly began to behave in ways unusual for peaceable Guwahati—road rage, drunk men harassing women, an aggression that didn't normally surface. Ved Ved crossed Keteki's mind for an instant. For all his flailing to impress when they'd first met, he'd seemed essentially harmless.

A few days later, it rained all night. When Keteki woke, it was still raining. She heard drums: the beginning of the immersion processions. From the window in the stairwell, she saw floats pass, sedate lorries bearing painted plaster idols of the goddess vanquishing the demon Mahishasura. People followed the floats, chanting and dancing. After breakfast, she went out to look at the float from Barowari. In the knot of people on the street were some of her relatives and friends. Pia waved at her.

Her friend Babu put an arm around her shoulders. 'When did you get back?' he asked. 'We haven't seen you.'

'I've barely left home,' Keteki said. 'Jet lag maybe.'

They followed the float, drummers dressed in white urging everyone on to dance. At Latasil, they turned the corner to skirt the playing field, and two bearded youths who looked like Calcutta University Marxists from the sixties danced forward into the road, dropped something and shimmied back. There was a deafening explosion.

'You'd think we would have had enough of this in the nineties,' murmured Keteki to the nearest person, who happened to be her aunt. Puwali pehi giggled.

At Fancy Bazar, the road widened, and other processions mingled with theirs. A little ahead, Keteki saw the river and remembered walking here, lovelorn, blinking back tears. But she was no longer that person. The river, blue and serene, bowled onwards. It had places to go, new names to assume: after crossing the border in Bangladesh, it would become the Jamuna, then the Meghna. Keteki felt a tiny release inside, as though in her heart a minuscule elastic band had snapped, an old moment of pain been released. She began to laugh. Nearby, Pia caught the mood. 'Look,' she said. Their own float was passing them. It made a U-turn and approached the river bank. They walked closer. The air was thick with Hindi music from huge loudspeakers. A set of pipes spewed festive red powder. Through the crimson mist, they gazed on the bright, indefatigably cheerful face of this year's goddess for the last time before she teetered down to the water.

3

The thing

'THIS IS ON ME,' Ved said.

'Excellent,' said Graham. 'Let's eat, I'm starving.'

Ved stared at Graham, who was consuming scallop ceviche. Ved was so anxious he felt he'd die if he had to wait another minute to speak.

Graham looked up. 'So,' he said, and smiled.

'The thing is,' said Ved.

The waiter appeared, interesting Graham in caperberries. Ved pushed prosciutto around a small plate.

'There's this woman,' he said. 'I met her in India. Or actually on the plane on the way there. Now I want to see her again.'

Graham smiled. 'You met someone!'

Ved pulled at his collar, though he wasn't wearing a tie. 'I met her in September. I can't stop thinking about her. She's beautiful, intelligent—sort of completely calm?'

Graham looked surprised. 'You met her in September? Two months ago? Have you been chatting?' He mimed texting with his thumbs.

'Well—not that much. A bit.' Ved waved at the waiter for another drink.

'Oh.'

'But, you know, the first time we met, we went out and spent the night together.'

'Okay. So it must have gone well?'

'How do you mean?' Ved became aware that if he leaned any further across the table, he'd be in the ceviche.

'You know. Did she seem happy?'

Ved exhaled. 'I thought so. But now I'm not sure. I thought she was amazing, so maybe I didn't, you know … notice what she seemed to feel.'

'You haven't been in touch with her since?'

'I text her,' said Ved. 'I want to go and see her. As soon as possible. The thing is …'

'She hasn't said yes?' Graham began to scan the menu.

'She hasn't said no,' Ved said. He looked away, at a couple of girls in bandage dresses at the bar. They had nice arses and everything. But all he wanted was to look at Keteki, maybe as she slid him a sideways look along the ramparts of her cheekbones. His stomach lurched.

'I have her number,' Ved said. 'And there's this client, the light bulb thing. One of their factories is in Assam, where she lives. So I thought …'

Graham laughed. 'Stalking is always an option,' he said.

'I—' said Ved. He realised he'd pulled up his collar, and hastily folded it down. 'The thing is,' he said, 'I haven't really been out with anyone for that long. Since college, actually. I can't remember what people do to start a relationship. And I don't think I made a very good job of that one. I ran into my ex-girlfriend once in Heathrow, and she looked like she hated me.'

'Well,' said Graham, 'that was twenty years ago. Presumably you've … you know?'

'Seventeen years,' corrected Ved. 'What?'

'You must have grown up a bit since then?'

Ved gave this some thought. Eventually he said, 'Does anyone really grow up?'

'Mate.'

'Right, right.'

In his flat that night, Ved undid the string on his laundry parcel. He looked at his clean, pressed shirts. He ran the tap and drank some filtered water, looked at the bottles near the cooker, and wondered if anyone had successfully overdosed on balsamic vinegar. He sat on the couch, put up his feet and looked out of the window. The night was wet. A drunk man passed outside and sobbed loudly, 'Oh! It hurts, it hurts.' He didn't seem to be talking about a physical pain, and the sound of a human being being human chilled Ved. It said: you may not get what you want.

4

Coffee break

KETEKI SAT ON her mat, stretched out her right leg, bent the left knee, hooked her left arm around it from the front, her right arm from the back, held the right hand in the left, straightened her back, and bent forward. She focused on the ache in her hamstring as, slowly, it began to open.

But even when her yoga was done, she was antsy. She picked up her phone to call Sumit.

'Hi. Are you busy? I was thinking of dropping in. Eleven-thirty? No issues, I have work after that too. See you then.'

Sumit was tall and lanky. His posture made him look like a rubber man, bending around the middle. 'Hi!' he said. 'How're *you*?' He smiled widely. 'Come in, come in, come in, the maid just left, so everything is a bit less of a mess, ha ha.'

The house in the forested railway colony was ramshackle and open, books and journals everywhere, wooden chairs on the veranda.

'Do you want some tea or anything?' he offered. 'Or coffee. I can ...'

Keteki put her keys on the hall table. 'Just water,' she said. She drank it, put the glass on a coaster, and walked into

Sumit's bedroom, taking off her sunglasses and hair band, and shaking out her hair. She pulled her top over her head and was unbuttoning her jeans when Sumit pulled her to him. He squeezed one of her breasts, then grabbed her bum and helped her out of her jeans. Usefully, he already had a hard-on. He removed his own shirt and pants, and she sat on the unmade bed for a second till he stretched over her and started to kiss her neck, then put a nipple in his mouth.

'Mm. Just—' she said, holding his cock and moving her hand.

'Ah,' he said, his mouth full of breast.

'I don't—'

Sumit lifted his head. 'Calm down,' he said, a little aggrieved. 'We're getting there. Are you in a big hurry or something?'

'Sorry,' Keteki said. 'Just a bit twitchy.' She lay back and submitted to a couple of minutes of his licking her quite skilfully. The thing about men who prided themselves on being good in bed was that they'd never just go with what you wanted in the moment. Still, it could have been a lot worse.

Sumit's voice was soft and well bred. While he was inside her, lying behind her and fucking her as he held her hips and she touched her clitoris, he murmured a gentle but persistent narrative. 'You're so wet, and you're so turned on. You're going to come so hard you'll have come running down your thighs and you'll put on your jeans and go home wet. You're going to come to my office and I'm going to fuck you on the desk. How am I going to fuck you?'

Keteki got distracted, wondering if he felt come should be spelt c-u-m, a convention that had always distressed her. However, she responded politely, 'You're going to lay me on the desk and fuck me from behind.'

He moved a little faster, holding her by one shoulder and one hip. His body was warm and companionable; she could feel he was turned on by her pleasure as well as what he was imagining. Still—

'Hang on,' she said. 'Go on top of me. No, lean your weight on me.' They repositioned, and she lifted her hips to push against him. 'Mm,' she said. 'Slower. Yes.'

A while later, she had her arm under her head and was smelling either herself or the air, sweaty and musky. 'Your room smells like fucking,' she said.

Sumit laughed. 'Well, better than smelling like Xeroxed test papers for once,' he said. 'I miss smoking. The post-fuck ciggie used to be great.'

Keteki fell asleep, and woke when she heard the shower. She got up as Sumit came out of the bathroom. Sunlight, the open window, the huge papery dusty leaves of a xaal tree outside and a cake of soap that smelled of oranges. Once dressed, she found Sumit in the kitchen.

'Good to see you,' she said, preparing to leave.

'Have a cup of coffee,' he said, a little hurt. 'I have to go to work afterwards too.'

'All right,' Keteki said.

It was part of Sumit's courtliness to insist on the cup of coffee, the conversation, as though to prove that they were friends. She sat sipping the coffee, which was instant and soapy.

Sumit waved the newspaper at her. 'Did you see this? All these supposed financial clean-ups. My ass.' He shook his head, stretched his arm out on the table. 'All the claims the government is making about cleaning up corruption. For example, consider the business of apparently cracking down on income tax. What rubbish. Do you know how many people in this country of over a billion declare an income of over a crore?'

Keteki looked at him. His voice had become louder, more rhetorical. She half smiled. Had she met him now, surely she would never have had sex with him. In fact, she couldn't remember why they began sleeping together, except that she liked him and he was neither chauvinist nor bad in bed.

'Do you know?' he repeated.

'You're talking to me as though I were one of your students. No, I don't know.'

'Forty-eight thousand. And how many declare over five crore rupees?'

Keteki shrugged. 'I don't know,' she said. 'Do tell me.'

'Three thousand. Is that even fucking believable?' He stared at her indignantly.

'Not at all.'

'So that's the situation. It's absurd. What the government says has a kind of … soap-opera relationship to what's actually going on.'

'You're right,' Keteki said. She smiled out of the open back door, at the sunshine, the magenta bougainvillea, a fat xaalika hopping on the railing of the veranda and chirruping in the winter sun. 'I'll head off now, Sumit. Thanks for coffee.'

'I'm going too,' he said, and she felt a vague irritation at having waited. Whenever she really listened to someone else, she'd become almost hyperattentive to the other person, who often urged her to stay a little longer than she happened to want to. While Sumit had been talking, she had the sense that, in her presence, he simply liked himself a little more than usual. Naturally, he wanted to prolong the experience.

Moments later, she was in the car, driving towards Jalukbari. The windows were open; dust came in from the flyover. Keteki drove straight under it, and started to think about lunch. Finally, her body was floppy, unknotted.

5

Milk jug

IN THE AFTERNOON, cold and sleepy, Keteki went online and posted a picture of the milk jug from the Arts and Crafts at Home exhibition, with a caption about where the jug had been made and what they knew of its history. She gazed at the jug for a minute. It was plain, porcelain, glazed a soft grey, with a single ridge around the body; it seemed to know how to be exactly what it was.

The afternoon passed slowly, and Keteki went through her bank statements, compiled a list of receipts and expenses, made an appointment to meet her accountant the following week and tried to concentrate on her emails. The milk jug had forty-three likes. Mark Hannon, a friend from London, was emailing to ask what her plans were the following year; he might have some work for her to collaborate on. Her phone buzzed. Ved was starting an amorous conversation. She replied, and wandered through to the drawing room to turn on the television, flicking channels, first pausing at an Assamese news channel showing footage of a woman harassed on the street in Pan Bazar. She had fought back, hitting her attacker on the head with her handbag. Then a Hindi news channel,

something about a Muslim man in Uttar Pradesh who had
been beaten to death by a Hindu mob accusing him of having
eaten beef. Another Assamese channel, and the tail end of a
report about an incident in upper Assam at a factory where
two groups of workers had had a dispute about the shrine on
the premises. There was a photo of the shrine and a goddess
idol, more like a doll with a many-pointed star on her brow.
The lettering above her said Phiringoti Devi Mandir. Goddess
of sparks? But you could make a shrine to anything. She
thought she recognised the logo on the factory sign—a little
devil with a spark on his tail.

Sunset came early, and it was soon dark. She carried on
with her work, went out for a walk, and to the market for
groceries. In the evening, Ranbir, an old friend, phoned to
say there was a party at his house. 'Just close friends,' he said.
'Why don't you come over?'

It was a typical Guwahati party: a few people in the living
room, the kitchen door open, more people smoking and
talking on the balcony. Ranbir gave Keteki a hug, took from
her the beer she'd brought and went to get her a cold one.
Someone else appeared and put an arm around her shoulder.
'Keteki Sharma! Where have you been?'

'Hey Mridul. So good to see you.' He had put on weight,
and looked hollow-eyed. 'How was your bike trip?'

'Amazing memory!' He began to tell her about the
motorcycle tour to Bhutan that he'd done soon after the last
time they'd met, and she was nodding and smiling by the time
Ranbir came back with a glass of beer. Keteki patted Mridul
on the arm, saying, 'I so admire how adventurous you are.'

Ranbir gave her a dry look. 'Hey, Lily and Mary are here
as well, and they're making pork curry and fish curry too.'

'Amazing,' Keteki said, though she planned, as always, to go home and raid the fridge for dail-bhaat. There was nothing like simple food, eaten at home, even at two in the morning, before crawling into bed.

'*Hi*, Ketu,' said a litte girl's voice, rather put out.

'Hey Tara,' said Keteki. 'You look great.'

They smiled at each other, Keteki with amusement, Tara with some pique. She was a Guwahati party fixture, famous for wearing tiny shorts whenever appropriate, and sometimes when not. This evening she had on quite a lot of make-up. After scanning Keteki, who was wearing a sweater and jeans, Tara relaxed. Keteki smirked, imagining Tara reassuring herself, '*I'm* still the hottest girl here.'

'Where are you back from this time, Ketu? You always seem to be somewhere exotic.'

'Scotland,' Keteki said.

'So lovely! Shillong is the closest most of us get to Scotland.' She laughed at her own joke. 'And where's Sumit these days? Isn't he with you today?'

'No idea where he is,' said Keteki, bored. Tara asked her about every man she'd been seen with, perhaps hoping Keteki would just get a boyfriend and stop being so annoyingly available. Everyone's life is ridiculous, Keteki thought, grinning as she remembered being at the candlelit market in Uzan Bazar earlier, shopping for vegetables and fruit, and stopping for a minute to reply to one of Ved's sexts. She'd been standing next to a vegetable stall on the edge of the market, typing something about how she was going down on Ved and sucking his hard cock when she'd looked down to see a goat munching cabbage leaves near her foot. Now, she looked at Tara in her playsuit and little heels and thought that, by the law of opposites, things always being exactly not what they seemed, Tara was probably in a super steady relationship so boring it was virtually a marriage.

Near midnight, Keteki found herself with a plate of fish curry and rice, sitting on the sofa next to a quiet young man in faded jeans and a grey T-shirt. She introduced herself.

'Clive,' he said, holding her hand very briefly.

'Try the fish curry?' Keteki said.

'Oh, thanks, but I'm vegetarian.'

'No kidding? Where are you from?'

He smiled. 'I'm half Bengali, half Naga.'

'Wow.'

While she ate, Keteki asked him questions about where he lived, and what he was doing in Guwahati. He said he was passing through, and that he and some friends ran a group they called the Pigeon Post, taking supplies to remote villages in Arunachal, near the border with China, the kind of places without electricity. 'Lamps, supplies, books, all kinds of things that people ask for,' he said. His voice was very quiet. Keteki had rarely met someone who projected outwards less. 'I do a lot of travelling,' he said. 'I don't live in any one place.'

While he talked, she saw images of treks through the mountains, tiny rope bridges across deep valleys, a jeep filled with supplies, a dusty village where, in the evening, a filament in a light bulb danced for the first time. 'I met someone a couple of months ago, who was working with a light bulb factory in upper Assam. Maybe you can get them to help you with sponsorship or something,' she said.

Clive blinked. 'Well, we don't really work with companies, except if someone makes a donation or offers us materials. But I wouldn't rule out anything. None of this was ever planned, you know. It was the way I was living anyway, coming together with doing this, it just evolved.'

'I envy you,' Keteki said. 'Maybe it sounds crazy, but I never think of my life that way, as just one thing. It always feels like separate parts: Assam and outside, work and friends.' She shrugged.

Clive had begun to say something when Keteki's phone rang. She took it out: Niki.

'It's a friend's younger brother,' she said. 'My friend died several years ago, but I'm still close to his brother.' Before she left the party, she took Clive's number. Maybe she'd go with him on one of those long trips to a village in the mountains. No—but he was a talisman against something, the repetition of more evenings like this.

A few hours later, she said, 'Niki … you know this isn't a great idea, don't you?' She caressed his head.

'I love you, Ketu,' said Niki contentedly.

She lifted her head from his shoulder and looked into his young face, touched his cheek with a finger. A phrase returned to her from somewhere, 'pure like a mirror'.

'You're glowing, you know,' he said. 'There's light coming out of your face.'

'Funny thing to say.'

'Funny, why?'

'I don't know,' she said. 'It reminds me of something. Niki, listen.' She sat up and looked at him. 'You know I love you too, but not that way. I'm not going to be your girlfriend or something. I'm sure there are other people who'd like to be, though.'

He laughed and got up to pee. 'One or two maybe,' he said, the door open, 'but why would I settle for one of them?'

Keteki woke at five o'clock. Outside, dogs were howling, sounding like they were auditioning for a horror film. She lay still for a while, investigating the corners of her awareness. Niku snored quietly. It was true, she did love him, but without attachment. She couldn't remember what it felt like to be in love, or why people wanted to entangle themselves. Was there something wrong with her? She got up, found her clothes, and went into the bathroom to clean her teeth, a dot of toothpaste on her finger. In the mirror, she saw her face, blank as a child's.

As she drove home she contemplated the streets, bathed in sunrise, here and there a homeless person dishevelled but gilded. The light was like nowhere else, as though filtered: an illustration of what light meant.

6

Guwahati

WHEN VED WOKE, the plane was descending. Out of the window, he saw hills, forest, a small river, then a huge river, shimmering metallic. Green fields, ponds, palm trees.

Half an hour later, he was being driven into town, in the back of a white Ambassador, past a university campus, featureless in the smoggy afternoon. As soon as he checked into the guesthouse in Uzan Bazar, he dialled Keteki's number and listened to the phone ring.

That evening, as dusk fell, he went for a walk. In the small street of the main market, he saw the flare of oil lamps and candles, illuminating baskets filled with different things: a pumpkin, cut open, some kind of green-striped squash, small fish, their scales flashing silver. Further on, he passed the High Court, and a large temple, a footbridge and many ragged beggars. The riverbank came into view, the water covered with a thick mist. There was a sudden dissonant fanfare from behind Ved—he jumped onto the pavement. A green and white bus. The conductor hung out of the back, beckoning to Ved. 'Jalukbari, Jalukbari!' he urged. 'Beltola?'

Ved shook his head. Rackety, shuddering, the bus farted warm fumes into the cold air and shot into the traffic.

Keteki phoned the next day and suggested a walk by the river. 'It's lovely in the evening,' she said. 'We'll go by four, before it's dark.'

She met Ved outside the guesthouse, smiling but matter of fact. 'Hi, Ved! What a surprise to get your message. Here, let's go this way,' she said, and crossed the main road to head up the lane opposite.

Ved just about avoided an auto rickshaw, a cycle rickshaw and two boys on a scooter. He hurried to keep up with Keteki. She looked good, but different—she clearly hadn't dressed up, and wore jeans, canvas hi-tops, and a jumper big enough that originally it must have belonged to some man. Her hair was up, a line of smoke under her eyes.

'It's so great to see you,' he said a bit resentfully, and nearly bumped into her. She had stopped to say hello to a bulldog cross outside a green wood-framed house. The dog eyed Ved as though he were biteable and barked.

'Stop it, Tyson,' said Keteki, bending down to hug the dog.

'You know each other, I see,' said Ved.

She shrugged and smiled. Then she was off again.

'You walk fast,' Ved said.

She shot him a look over one high cheekbone. 'I feel it's important to camouflage my natural aimlessness, Ved.' They were at the bigger road that ran along the river. 'So how have you *been*?' She touched his elbow. 'Let's cross?'

They did, just as a moped with two teenagers on it shot past. Ved made an inadvertent lunge towards Keteki.

'Are you *okay*, Ved?'

He dusted off his shoulder, and climbed onto the high pavement to join her. Behind iron fencing, then trees, he caught a glimpse of the river, azure blue. 'Really, it's great to see you,' he said. 'I—' But he had to move out of the way of two burly women in salwar kameez and trainers who were walking in the opposite direction.

'It gets very *busy* in the evening,' Keteki murmured. 'I thought we'd see the sunset, walk up towards the Governor's house maybe.' She slowed down. 'So what do you think of Guwahati?'

'I haven't seen much. It's beautiful. The river. Uh, I didn't really see it yesterday, there was a heavy mist ...' Ved was following her again, down off the pavement, then up. Lower down the bank there was an area of covered stalls, the remnants of a fish market, smelling very much like a fish market.

'That's the fish market,' explained Keteki.

'I see that,' said Ved. 'I guess the boats land here.' He peered at the bank.

'Sort of,' she said.

'Sort of?'

'Well, they do land here, and they bring fish, but most of it is farmed in north Guwahati. The other bank.'

'Oh.'

'Yes, very authentic,' Keteki said.

Ved told her about the Lucifer. He was to go to upper Assam to visit the factory—a Mr Banerjee would show him around. Ved would take the train to Jorhat tomorrow.

'Jorhat?' said Keteki. 'That's my place. My uncle lives there, in our family house. My mother's family, that is. On my father's side, the main person I spend all my time with is my aunt, here in Guwahati.' She paused. They had come to a ravine. At the bottom, a rivulet joined the Brahmaputra. But the sides of the ravine were lined with refuse: plastic plates, shit, tampons, cigarette packets, matchboxes, everything. A man stood on the side, pissing. Ved looked at him, then away. The place stank.

'I know,' Keteki said. 'But maybe it's edifying to see all the filth on the surface. Sad for the river though. There are so many people who live in this area now, in what used to be railway land. Some of the old families here are quite angry about all this.'

They passed some small shops and began to walk up the hill, the sweep of river on one side, the sun flaring red as it slipped down.

'Are you free for dinner tonight?' Ved asked.

'Dinner?'

'I mean, would you like to have dinner with me?'

Keteki looked at him sidelong. She smiled. 'Oh, that's so sweet of you, Ved. But dinner's a long time away. I was supposed to meet some people—friends. Why don't I give you a call or something? They're great guys. Oh look. I *like* these two.' She pointed at a pair of street dogs, one sandy, one white. As the hill curved and rose, there were teenagers in cars and on motorbikes parked near the pavement, playing music loudly and flirting. 'It's a bit of a hangout, as you can see,' Keteki said. 'Let's walk up till the Raj Bhawan.' Her legs took the slope easily; Ved toiled beside her, feeling jet-lagged and unfit.

'Is there somewhere we can stop and sit down?' he asked.

'Actually, Ved,' she said confidingly, 'don't think I'm a terrible host, but I need to finish some work. Would you mind? I know you've come all the way from London.' She paused, turned to him and smiled.

'God, no,' said Ved eagerly. 'I mean, I know I just surprised you out of the blue.'

'So great to see you, Ved. I'm really looking forward to spending some time together.' They came back down the slope, and she took his arm. 'Listen, I have one or two things to do, but you can get back to your guest house by going straight down here and taking the first left. Do you remember? Walk to the end of the lane and cross the main road and you'll be there. Will you be all right?'

'Don't worry,' Ved said quickly. 'Will I see you later? It's just that my train is first thing in the morning.'

'Of course, Ved. I'll call you soon. We'll make a plan. I wish I'd known you were going to Jorhat. I'd love to see my uncle. Let's see if I can get away.' She was already waving as she walked off.

7

Jorpukhuri

UNDER FLUORESCENT LIGHT, Ved was sitting down to eat in the guest house at nine-thirty when the phone in his pocket buzzed. It was a local landline. Ten minutes later, dinner abandoned, he was standing in the porch of a cream-coloured house a few streets away. He rang the doorbell and braced himself for an elderly aunt.

Keteki opened the door.

'You made it,' she said cheerfully.

'I did. I hope I'm not disturbing anyone,' Ved said. He followed her in.

'My aunt's out,' Keteki said. 'Anyway, we're going out soon. Just sit down for a minute. I'll order a cab, it's easier than driving.'

While he waited, Ved wandered around the living room. There was good old wooden furniture, and framed photographs on the wall. A little girl, with two plaits, smiling at the camera; a thin, handsome man with a charming smile and good hair in a ridiculous pair of bell-bottoms; a strikingly beautiful woman, her presence uncertain, something angry in her smile. Other relatives: a young woman, cheerful in what looked like a sari; an older couple.

'The cab's here, I think,' said Keteki, behind Ved. 'Shall we?'

'It's a lovely house,' he said, as she was locking the door, insects whirling about the porch light.

'It's— Yes, it's the family house in Guwahati. We don't live in all of it, the upper floor is rented to tenants. A nice couple, social anthropologists. She's German, but speaks perfect Assamese. Of course they'll only be here for six months or so. Family property is so complicated.' Keteki shrugged. 'The house belongs to my father's siblings, but of the three surviving ones, one is in America and one in Bangalore. No one wants to sell it, but no one apart from my aunt wants to live in it.' She ran down the steps to the quiet lane where a white car was waiting, engine running. A large moon glared in the sky. Keteki said something to the driver, who smiled and nodded. They got in the back.

'What would you say is your biggest fear, Ved?'

'My biggest fear?' Ved laughed unsuccessfully. 'Um.'

'Tell the truth,' Keteki invited. He could smell her perfume, heady and smoky.

Ved cleared his thought. He saw again the inside of the house in Hounslow where he'd grown up, bad lighting, his mother in a bad mood. 'Well,' he said. 'I guess just fucking everything up.'

'That's a bit general, nai?'

'Erm,' Ved said. 'You know, turning out to be, well, useless. Pathetic. A waste of space.' The image of his mother's angry face reappeared, and he turned his head.

The taxi skirted a large pond, with small houses around it, looking as though it were in a small village somewhere, rather than in the city.

'This is Jorpukhuri, two ponds together. See, the pond on the right belongs to the temple, it's very old. The one on the left is a favourite for people committing suicide.'

'What?'

'Really. Even several members of my family through the generations.'

'I—'

'Useless, did you say?' she continued in her clear voice.

'Well,' said Ved. They passed some small shops, a brightly lit café. The remark about suicide must have been a joke. 'I mean, doesn't everyone fear something similar?'

Keteki considered. The taxi swung onto a main road. 'No, my biggest fear probably is repeating the same mistake, over and over,' she said.

The taxi began to climb a flyover, lit in acid yellow. Everything looked unreal. Ved took Keteki's hand. 'I'm sure you're not going to do that,' he said. She leaned forward to tell the driver something. They continued on the large road and took a left at a traffic light. There was an SUV parked by the roadside.

'This is where we're going?'

'Just meeting some friends,' Keteki said. She pulled out her phone, thanked the driver and got out. Ved followed.

A knot of men, their breath making vapour clouds in the cold air, turned as they approached. There was a roar. 'Ketu!' said the tallest, wrapping her in a hug.

Keteki smiled up at him. He was wearing a hoodie. 'Bips!' she said, putting her hands on his large upper arms.

'Hi?' said Ved behind her.

'Sorry, Bips,' Keteki said. 'This is my friend Ved, visiting from London. Ved, Bips is a very old friend.'

'Ketu,' Bips was saying. 'You look younger every time I see you. What's happening?'

'But I don't actually look the way I used to when I was younger,' Keteki pointed out. 'I look like someone else.'

'That's true.' Bips gazed into her face. 'So who the hell are you?'

They both laughed. Keteki released one hand from Bips's arm and looked at Ved over her shoulder.

'Ved, sorry,' said Bips. 'We all love this woman.'

'Of course,' said Ved.

The door of the SUV was open, and loud music blasted out in some dialect of Hindi. Keteki raised an eyebrow. 'Bips, what is this music?' she asked.

Another man, younger and fair-skinned, leaned out of the car. 'Hello, Ketu ba.'

Keteki went up to him. 'Tito, is this your Punjabi side? Do you have something more mellow? For us old people?'

Tito, who was wearing a padded gilet and polo shirt, a pair of aviators propped on his shorn head, smiled. 'Retro?' he suggested.

Keteki leaned against the door. Other cars passed in the cold evening, using their horns. One or two groups walked past on their way to the Chinese restaurant on the first floor in the building behind them.

'Ved, here.' Bips reached inside the car and passed Ved a water bottle. Ved looked at him. 'Have some, Ved.'

Ved took a gulp and coughed.

Keteki took a sip. 'What's the mixer?'

'Sprite.'

'Too sweet,' she said, shaking her head.

'Cheers,' said Ved. 'So, um, we were going to go for dinner. I don't know what you guys are planning?'

Keteki smiled at him from the side of the vehicle. 'Let's be here for some time,' she said. 'Some more people are on their way.'

A while later, another car drew up, and three men got out. One of them, tall and friendly, gave Keteki a hug.

'Rishi,' said Keteki. To Ved, she said, 'This is my cousin, Adim. His pet name is Rishi. Rishi, Ved is from London.'

'London!' His surprise was theatrical. 'When did you come down to Guwahati?'

'Well, I landed on the eighth,' Ved said. 'I'm going to upper Assam tomorrow.'

'Upper Assam! Wow, this guy is really getting around,' said Adim, looking impressed. 'Most foreigners barely make it to the northeast but you're going to upper Assam. Tell me more?'

While Ved was filling Adim in on his trip, and Adim was explaining to Ved that a group of friends standing around one or two cars and drinking all evening was a classic Guwahati night out, Keteki was talking to Sumit, laughing and sharing a cigarette. Gutli, a short, balding man, appeared with two paper plates of dumplings. 'Momos!' cried everyone. The glistening dumplings were filled with pork and onion. Ved ate one, and became aware that he'd drunk a lot on an empty stomach.

Some time later, they were all in the two cars, careening in the direction of some place called Paltan Bazar, where they said they'd be able to buy more alcohol. The streets were midnight blue, with flashes of sulphur yellow; not a dog moved; the car lurched on the road and the driver giggled. Ved sat in the back next to Keteki, and Sumit and Gutli were on pull-out seats. Gutli was telling Keteki a story about his aunt.

'She started sending me these crazy texts, dei,' he said. '"Where's my money", that sort of thing.'

'Oh, really,' said Keteki.

'But did you borrow money from her?' asked Sumit.

'No!'

'Oh, crazy, man.'

'I mean,' said Gutli, 'you know, like ten *years* earlier.'

Keteki giggled.

'She's my favourite aunt,' Gutli complained. 'Why doesn't she understand?'

At Paltan Bazar, outside a hotel that was closed, some of the men went to a hole in the wall to buy more booze. Ved, explaining that he didn't smoke, asked where he could get cigarettes and was pointed in a direction. He wandered down a lane that smelled of pee. A bit later, he came back looking for the car. He couldn't find the others. He tried to phone Keteki just before his battery died.

8

The ends of the earth

THE TRAIN WAS freezing. Ved shivered in the air-conditioned compartment, and looked out of the window at a boy wrapped in a huge shawl, sitting on the platform. The boy's breath made a cloud. The train started. Ved pulled his jacket around him and slept, dreaming on and off of the preceding hours, when he'd wandered around for ages, trying to find a rickshaw, then slowly finding his way back to Uzan Bazar. Near the river, he drank tea made by a Bihari man who grilled him. No, he wasn't married. Yes, he was from abroad. Yes, he would like more tea. Yes, a biscuit too. He'd made it back to the guesthouse just in time to have a quick wash, change his clothes and dash back to Paltan Bazar for the train.

At Dimapur, an influx of shrieking students boarded the train. Ved gave in to the tea seller, and drank several cups of tea, milky, and not as good as the fragrant red tea at the riverside. He stared through the yellow-tinted windows at the countryside: green fields, sometimes half-flooded, people dressed in white bending over small paddy plants; a few houses here and there, then rows of dark green plants bounded by trees. Those must be the tea estates. It was odd how oppressive they looked.

The train passed through stops: Furkating, Mariani Junction. A while later, it pulled into an undramatic, dusty station. Everyone began to get off. Soldiers came to meet what must been army wives, who indicated their bags. Ved picked up his holdall and sloped out.

'Ved!'

He flinched.

A tall, handsome man beamed at him. 'Rajen Banerjee, from the Lucifer factory. How was your journey? My jalopy is just outside.' He patted Ved on the shoulder.

Mr Banerjee was not a small man, and the car was not large. He flicked Ved's holdall into the boot, got in and opened the passenger door. 'It's a nice drive,' he said. 'But tell me. You must be hungry?'

They set off, and as the car rattled through the town, Ved looked out at the dusty road and shops with their wares displayed outside: plastic piping, nozzles, buckets, mops, fruit, winter clothing, woollen hats.

Rajen was talking about the options for lunch. 'I know a really *good* place. Fish, chicken too. Would you have liked pork though, Ved? You aren't,' and he blanched a little, 'a veget*arian*, are you?'

'No, no,' said Ved. 'Brought up vegetarian, but I eat everything.' He looked out of the window. 'There seems to be a lot of construction going on.'

'Yes, Ved, they're widening the road. It'll become a four-lane expressway. You've come to the most historic part of Assam, you know. But I'm sure you know all about that.'

'Not really,' Ved said. He was tired and hungry. 'I don't know anything.'

Rajen waved a large hand. 'Well,' he said. 'Assam was ruled for six centuries by the Ahoms, a tribe from southeast China.

We owe a lot of our culture to that. The Ahoms became
Hindus after a while, but they had their own religion, their
own language. There are still some Tai Ahom settlements,
you know, in upper Assam.' He waved a hand. 'But for the
most part they're assimilated. They used to be the rulers,
now they're a minority.' He smoothed his moustache. 'The
caste Hindus also came from elsewhere, originally—Bihar, the
north, Bengal.'

'Isn't your name Bengali?' Ved asked.

Rajen nodded. 'My father's family,' he said. 'My mother's
family is Assamese. But even my father's family would have
been here for generations. No one remembers where we came
from.'

'Really?' Ved looked longingly at the roadside restaurants
they passed, and wondered if Keteki had tried to call him
at some point while his phone was off or out of range. For
a while he'd thought last night was going well, but it had
dissolved into chaos. He hoped she'd worried about him.

'This whole area has seen so many movements of people
through the ages,' Rajen was saying. 'The original inhabitants
are from the Tibeto-Burman tribes.' He waved a hand. 'Like
the Bodos today, or the Khasis in Meghalaya.' He kept talking,
and Ved nodded when it seemed like time for a response.

Eventually they arrived at the restaurant. It was a large
low structure, not unlike a hangar, by the road. But inside, the
single room was lined with highly varnished split bamboo.
Pointed straw hats and white-and-red scarves decorated the
walls. 'What are those?' Ved asked. 'I've seen them in a few
places now.'

'Jaapi, Ved. Traditional straw hat, for working outdoors.'
Rajen mimed the act of covering his head. 'And the gamusa,

of course. In fact, remiss of me. I should have put one around your neck when I met you at the station.'

'My neck?' said Ved, startled.

Rajen laughed. 'Your shoulders. It's a traditional way of honouring a guest,' he said. 'Stringing you up with a gamusa wouldn't be in the spirit of Assamese hospitality at all.'

The waiter appeared.

'Bhaat aaru maas,' said Rajen. 'Beer?' he asked.

'Well,' Ved was beginning. Rajen nodded to the waiter. A cold bottle of beer and two glasses were brought.

'I didn't ask what you take,' Rajen said. 'Should have got some vodka, whisky, rum?' He cocked a melancholic eye at Ved.

'Maybe it's a bit early in the day—'

'Of course, of course. I have everything at my bungalow for the evening, Ved.'

His guest sighed. 'You were telling me about history,' he said.

'Well, the rule of the Ahoms was a time of great prosperity. They had a unique system of managing the people. Each man had the use of a plot of land, to grow what he needed for his family. We imported very little. And everyone had to render service to the army when required. There were officers in charge of the men. Those titles still survive in some of our common surnames today. A Bora was in charge of twenty men, a Saikia was in charge of a hundred, and so on. There were generals and priests and officials in charge of taming elephants, or procuring tamul, you know, betel nut, for the court.'

Ved realised he was drunk, and when a dish of small fried fish appeared, he needed little encouragement to try them.

They were spangled with slices of green chilli and onion, and were delicious.

Back in the car, in a post-rice, fish and beer haze, he managed to listen to some more of Rajen's narration while looking out at rice fields with mirror-like patches of flooding. The land was expansive, houses infrequent. At the horizon he saw shadowy blue hills. 'What are those?' he asked.

'The Patkoi mountains, Ved, in Nagaland. Do you remember how I was telling you about the Burmese invasion?'

Some time later, Ved woke up and quickly wiped his mouth. They had pulled in to another roadside restaurant. It was dark, a yellowish gleam in the moist blue night.

'Tea,' explained Rajen.

Ved sat blinking in the overly lit restaurant. 'Could we get some water?' he asked.

Rajen smiled. 'Headache?' he asked.

'I'm not much of a lunchtime drinker any more,' Ved said. 'Maybe the jet lag is catching up with me.' He thought of the previous night, which now seemed so far away, and winced. No news from Keteki. Maybe she had no interest in him, given the amount of interchangeable men she appeared to be surrounded by. He had a vision of many-headed demons in an Amar Chitra Katha, each of the many heads dark-skinned and with a splendid moustache, and looked at Rajen dubiously. 'You know, I may have fallen asleep for a bit in the car. Sorry. These lights might be giving me a bit of a headache, actually.'

Rajen laughed, a boom that turned into a high-pitched wheeze at the end. 'You were out like a light!' he said. 'Sleeping like a baby.'

Ved tried to smile, and pinched the fold between his eyebrows.

'You know,' Rajen said, 'we have a tube light in development. I'll be able to show you more at the plant.'

'Oh?'

'It's in development, it's a prototype,' Rajen said. Little cups of sweetened red tea arrived, and a bottle of water. 'We're calling it the Guru,' Rajen went on. 'It's for larger spaces, you know, where people assemble. We've started testing it out, including in a few local namghors. Do you remember what I was telling you about them?'

Ved dredged his mind. This was turning into a very long supervision. 'Uh, the Vaishnav saint,' he said.

'Xonkordeb, yes. Of course, to really understand his legacy, the best place to visit is Majuli, Ved. Do you know about Majuli?'

'No,' said Ved resignedly.

Rajen laughed. 'Let's get back in the car,' he said.

'I'd love to hear more about the factory,' Ved said. 'How many workers do you employ?'

Rajen pulled out of the parking lot. The road was dark now, large trees looming in at them from time to time. 'We have around forty men—mostly men, anyway—on the floor at one time. They work in three shifts. The factory is almost always running. Most of our production is the Lucifer now. We do have a certain amount of LEDs and CFLs, but as you know,' he said, swerving around a truck and speeding up to overtake it so that they just avoided a collision with another car, which let out an extended protest from the horn, 'most of the regular bulbs are produced in Chennai. Really, the way some people drive.'

Ved exhaled and let go of the side of his seat. 'Incandescents? Who still buys incandescents?'

'People in villages,' said Rajen. 'They're cheap, they're bright.' He hesitated. 'Look, Ved, there is another thing. You'd find out about this eventually. There have been some disputes, labour issues at the factory. We have people from different tribes working with us. Principally Morans and Mataks, and some tea tribes, a few Hajong. It's difficult to understand if you don't know the background. Actually, it's difficult to understand even if you do know a bit about the background. It's not like Guwahati here. The tribes have their own issues, and they've been campaigning to get their status changed, you know, be listed as Scheduled Tribes.' He looked at Ved. 'Are you following any of this?'

'Scheduled Tribes,' said Ved. 'Um, let me think. That's— no, I don't remember.'

'Our Constitution lists certain communities as Scheduled Castes and Scheduled Tribes with reserved status. They get preferential treatment for certain things—education, government jobs, for instance. The tribes in many states of the northeast have scheduled status, for example in Meghalaya and Mizoram. Many of the important tribes in Assam don't have that status, and, naturally, they feel that's unfair. And then there is also competition about who should be entitled to reservations.' Rajen decided that the car in front of them was going too slowly and let out a loud honk.

'Right,' Ved said. The back of his neck was cold. When would this journey end? He felt dehydrated and depressed. For some reason, he'd felt that Keteki had silently instructed him to follow her to the ends of the earth, and beyond. Guwahati had felt like the ends of the earth. This was beyond. Rajen was looking at him.

'Good man,' said the Assamese man. 'You're tired. We're nearly there, not too much longer now.'

Why, Ved wondered the next morning, did factories always smell of steel? Steel and ashes. He was hungover again. He shivered, and had a memory of Rajen clinking glasses with him and saying 'Bottoms up' after he'd poured Ved yet more Bhutanese whisky.

'Tea?' said Rajen. 'Or hair of the dog?' He winked.

Ved closed his eyes. 'Water, please.' While he waited, he tried to remember what Rajen had told him about the factory workers last night as they sat up before a very late dinner. The majority were Morans and Mataks. They were tribals who had been looked down on in mainstream Hindu society. In the sixteenth century, they had converted to the Vaishnavism brought to Assam by the saint Xonkordeb. Then a long story about one of the famous monasteries or xotros, where there was a religious leader, something about the name—Moamara, Mayamara.

'But the point,' Ved remembered Rajen saying in the dim light of the hanging lamp above the small table and two cane armchairs, where they drank until midnight, 'the point, Ved, is that there is a wound. This was a tribal kingdom before the caste Hindus arrived, and since then there's been a tension between the mainstream of Hinduism, with all the emphasis on caste, and tribal societies. Don't get me wrong, Ved.' The big man's shirtsleeves were rolled up, and he waved his large hands. 'I am not in favour of splitting up Assam into enclaves, Bodoland, et cetera et cetera. I don't know if I even think that would be a solution. Not long ago, the Asom Sahitya Sabha, Ved, the body of Assamese writers, very important in our culture, said that anyone should be defined as Assamese whose first language is Assamese. That caused controversy because it seemed to include those of Bengali descent, even the children of more recent immigrants from Bangladesh.'

More Bhutanese whisky had gone into Ved's glass. He remembered staring around the room from their gently illuminated corner, and seeing the yellow light gleam on the arm of a teak chair, the corner of a table. The room felt like a spaceship, mobile in time, as Rajen talked.

'But it's not just about the Bangladeshis. What about a Bodo or a Khasi? Their first language is not Assamese, but their own language. Are we saying the Bodos and Khasis in Assam do not belong here? The Bodos are the original inhabitants of this country. But even they probably came from central Asia. How far back should we go?'

'Who really knows where anyone comes from?' Ved had wondered aloud.

'Exactly, Ved. Exactly.' Rajen's enormous fist came down on the arm of the cane chair.

'So what's the solution?' Ved asked.

Rajen had frowned and seemed to slump. 'I don't know, Ved.'

Now, Rajen's secretary appeared with water for Ved, tea for her boss. The big man sipped enthusiastically through his moustache. 'Finished?' he asked. 'Let's go for the tour.'

As they followed the production line, from the corner of his eye, Ved seemed to see a tiny flash. He rubbed his eyes and caught sight of a woman wearing a bright striped cloth, red, yellow and turquoise, wrapped over a white blouse. She was standing at a rubber conveyor belt, checking the bulbs that appeared before they went on to be boxed. Ved felt strange. The hangover, no doubt. There were trees around the factory, he saw when they emerged; their leaves were huge but dusty. He was trying to remember something he'd been meaning to ask Rajen.

There were a couple of men unloading boxes from a forklift. They nodded at Rajen and smiled at Ved. Rajen barked things at them and continued to walk on.

'And this,' he said, as they rounded a corner where there were a few sheds, more dusty, dark trees, and the sound of something scurrying on fallen, papery leaves, 'is a funny thing, but very important. Our factory temple.'

'Temple?'

'Yes, Phiringoti Devi. Everyone passes through here on their way in. In fact, recently some of the workers had a dispute about who was in charge of the temple. It may seem silly to you, Ved, but she's seen as something of a lucky mascot for us.'

Ved peered into the small cement building, like a large doll's house. Inside was a figure resembling a doll of a young, beautiful woman. Her skin was yellow, her eyes cartoonishly large, black and slanting, her hair long and wavy. On her forehead was a star, and strings of flashing fairy lights decorated the opening of the structure.

Rajen put his hands together, bowed and reached inside. The ring finger of his large right hand suddenly approached Ved's third eye and a soft cold touch firmly pressed between his eyebrows. 'Tika,' said Rajen. 'Very important.' He repeated the gesture to make the mark on his own forehead.

'Now we'll go into the office and look at the Guru
prototypes I told you about,' Rajen said. They headed towards
the main entrance, Ved following the other man. He was
suddenly both lightened and excited, for at the moment of
receiving the tika, the phone in his pocket had buzzed. He
took it out. Keteki had sent a message, suggesting he stop over
in Jorhat for a night, at her uncle's house.

9

The shape shifters

'Hi. Um, hello. I'm Ved.'

Keteki's uncle, tall, grey-haired, smiled. 'Hello, Ved, welcome. Jayanta.' He shook Ved's hand and patted his shoulder with the other hand.

'I call him Joy mama,' said Keteki. She was behind her uncle, leaning in the doorway.

'Ketu's mother was my younger sister, Ved,' explained Jayanta. 'But please, come in, come in.'

There was a hallway inside the porch, and a long corridor leading to other rooms, illuminated by a bare incandescent bulb hanging from the ceiling. Low bookshelves lined the passage. Something furry scurried past Ved's ankles. He looked back to see Keteki cooing in Assamese as she scooped up a fluffy marmalade cat.

'This is your room, Ved,' Jayanta was saying. 'I hope you'll be comfortable.' Ved followed him through a door. The room was filled with good wooden furniture. A chair near the foot of the bed had neatly folded towels on it.

'It's so kind of you to have me,' Ved said.

Keteki's uncle smiled. 'It's always good to have a guest, Ved. I'll let you freshen up. We'll have tea in about fifteen minutes.'

When Ved emerged from his room, having had a shower and shave and put on a clean shirt, he could hear Keteki's voice, at once recognisable but changed: still high and light, but happier, in interplay with her uncle's deeper voice. Ved walked through a book-lined drawing room and followed the voices through open French doors onto a veranda. Jayanta waved a hand. 'Bade, come, sit down, have some tea.'

Ved smiled at them. 'When did you get here?' he asked Keteki.

'Just a little before you. I left as early as I could, and arrived in time for a late lunch. It's so good to be here.' She stretched out contentedly.

'It's lovely here,' Ved said.

'The garden is at its best in summer,' Joy mama noted. 'But winter has its own charm. Ved, where are your people from? Gujarat?'

'Well, Kutch. But via Bombay,' Ved said. 'I don't have a large family. That is, my parents have been in England a very long time.'

Jayanta nodded. 'And this is your first visit to Jorhat?'

'Yes, absolutely,' Ved said. 'I mean, I took the train here to go to the factory. I don't know if Keteki mentioned it.' He turned to Keteki, for her uncle had winced. 'Am I mispronouncing your name horribly?'

The other two laughed. Keteki waved an extenuating hand. 'Only averagely,' she said.

Ved sighed. 'But in Assam you don't seem to pronounce the soft "t" and "d", is that right? So, in another part of India, it would be Keteki, soft "t", and here it's more like Ketecki.'

'And your name becomes Bade,' Keteki said.

'We do have the letters v, t, d, in our alphabet, Ved,' Joy mama said.

'We just prefer not to wear them out,' Keteki quipped.

Her uncle laughed. 'You, of course, are barely literate in your own language, because most of your education took place outside.' Keteki grinned at him.

'Ved,' Joy mama said, 'have a chicken sandwich. And try one of these puffs. Ketu, pass him the jam. Ved, this is made from a fruit called sohiong. We get it in Shillong, it's very good.' He bit into a chicken puff and leaned back.

'*What* are you eating?' Keteki enquired.

Her uncle looked slightly uncomfortable, but pleased with himself. 'I call this an assortiment de pain grillé,' he said. Ved laughed.

'Toast with peanut butter? Is that cheese spread? How much jam? What about your blood sugar?'

'Ketu,' said Joy mama reprovingly, 'it's not nice to be the kind of person who walks into a room and immediately spots the dust ball under the table. Your parents, all things considered, were at least charming people.'

Keteki smiled, then looked dreamy. 'Lachit Borphukan, I've always thought, had the right idea about how to deal with uncles,' she observed, eliciting a whinny of laughter from Joy mama.

'Good one,' he said.

'What?' Ved asked.

'Lachit Borphukan is our greatest Assamese general, Ved,' explained her uncle.

'In the Ahom period?' said Ved.

'Oho, you have been learning. I like him,' Joy mama said

to his niece. 'Yes. He defended Assam from the Mughals and turned them back at Saraighat, that's near Guwahati.'

'When the Assamese were preparing for battle, Lachit's uncle was in charge of a crew building a wall. They weren't working fast enough for Lachit, and his uncle said the men were tired. So Lachit chopped off the uncle's head. After that, everyone worked through the night.'

'Heavens,' said Ved.

'You see, Ved,' said Joy mama, 'we Assamese prefer not to work too *hard*. Of course there have been great soldiers, leaders, writers, what not, but on the whole,' and he waved a large hand, the finger tips a little spatulate, 'we are a *lazy* people. We like to take it easy.' He looked at his guest in a mute appeal for understanding.

'That sounds so nice,' Ved said with longing.

'Ida!' Keteki called out. Another cat, white and fluffy, approached, eyed them all balefully, and finally allowed her to pick it up and cuddle it.

'What's the cat's name?' Ved asked.

'This one is Ida, the other one is Pingala,' Keteki said.

'You know, like the sun and moon energies,' said Joy mama. Seeing from Ved's face that he didn't know, he chuckled. 'I used to be a bit of an eccentric, Ved. Yoga, studied abroad for a while, even turned vegetarian.'

'I see,' said Ved, not keeping up at all. Yoga? Sun and moon energies? Every time he got nearer to Keteki, instead of things becoming simpler, they became less comprehensible. What was he even doing here, in this extremely cultured house, with these baffling people?

Keteki's mouth curved, and he thought for a moment that she'd read his mind. 'I think Ved is a little jet-lagged,' she said to her uncle.

'Ved, so sorry. Never mind all this tea, let me get you a proper drink, and you can relax for a little bit before dinner,' Joy mama said. He got up. 'Come, come.'

'Is that all right?' Ved said. 'A drink sounds amazing. Although tea was lovely.'

'Sometimes, something a little stronger than tea hits the spot, if you know what I mean,' said Joy mama, setting forth into the room with the open French doors. When the others came in, he shut the doors and pulled crimson curtains across them.

'I'm going to take a bath, Ved,' Keteki said. 'It was a long drive. Make yourself at home and I'll see you in a bit.'

Ved looked around the room, lined with glass-fronted bookshelves from floor to ceiling. There were worn but good cane armchairs, a small table, a frayed Kashmiri carpet whose colours still glowed. 'Wow,' he said.

'We're all big readers,' said Joy mama. 'The problem becomes what to *do* with the books.' He put on a standard lamp that cast a beautiful, oddly humane light. Its shade looked unusual, like parchment. Joy mama went to a gramophone cabinet and opened the bottom with a small key. 'Here we are. Scotch, gin, rum, and some—' he fished out the bottle, looked at it, guffawed and handed it to Ved. 'What is this one, Ved? I can't see a damn thing. Age, you know.'

'It says Lindisfarne mead,' said Ved. 'This bottle must have travelled quite a way.'

'I haven't asked what you'd like, Ved,' said Joy mama. 'Whisky? Or would you prefer beer? We don't get good wine here, unfortunately. But there may be something in another cupboard.'

'Whisky would be great,' Ved said. 'Thanks so much.'

The older man rose and dusted his palms. He sneezed. 'This house is like an old person's skull,' he said, and grinned at Ved. 'Full of dust.'

Ved laughed.

'Tuku!' bellowed Joy mama.

'Sorry?'

'He'll just come, Ved.'

A young man appeared, slender in red T-shirt and a pair of trousers that his easy physicality made hipsterishly cool. 'Hello, I am Tuku,' he said, holding out a hand. Ved shook it; Tuku's handshake was brief and gentle.

'Ved. Nice to meet you,' said Ved, wondering who this was. A relative? He didn't resemble the other two. A servant? That didn't seem right either.

Joy mama patted Tuku's shoulder and said a few things in a tone somewhere between coaxing and gentle nagging. Tuku nodded and left the room, taking with him the dusty bottle of Scotch.

'Ved,' said Joy mama, 'I'll also go and clean up. Tuku will get you a drink. Sit down, relax. There's plenty to read if you feel like it.'

Left to himself, Ved scanned the shelves. Dictionaries, encyclopaedias, old magazines, books in English and Assamese. He studied the angular script. Wasn't it very like Bengali? He crouched at a lower shelf, then opened the glass door to remove a volume and went to sit in one of the armchairs near the French doors.

After a bit, Tuku returned with a tray—glasses, the whisky, ice, a soda siphon. He nodded at Ved. 'How are you?' he asked.

'I'm fine. How are you?'

'Very well.' He put down the tray. 'Shall I make your drink?'

'I'd like to do it, if you don't mind,' Ved said. He poured himself some whisky and added a little water.

'I'll bring a snack,' Tuku said.

'Don't worry,' Ved was beginning. 'Wait—'

Tuku returned.

'Are you—I don't know how you're related to Keteki and her uncle. I'm sorry, I don't know them well yet.'

Tuku's eyes, fine and dark, looked into Ved's. 'I look after the house, and I cook for Dada,' he said. 'I have been here since I was very young—very young.'

Ved felt he had never been so directly or comprehensively seen.

'I should carry on with the dinner,' Tuku said.

'Of course,' Ved said.

Joy mama returned soon, having changed his shirt. 'So sorry, Ved,' he said. 'We are treating you very badly, behaving like people in a Restoration comedy, always rushing offstage.' He grinned at the joke, and examined the table, where Ved's drink was. 'Tuku!'

Tuku appeared with a tray of fried things. 'O, Dada?' he said gently.

'Oh, he's brought you snacks. Lovely. Ved, these are all for you. My niece will kill me if I eat such things. I might join you in a drink, however.' He and Tuku had a short exchange and Tuku left again.

'What are you reading, Ved?' Joy mama helped himself to whisky, water and ice.

Ved turned the cover to face him: *Assam and the Assamese Mind.*

'Ha!' said Joy mama. 'Nagen Saikia's book. So you want to know about the Assamese mind?'

'It seemed like a good idea,' mumbled Ved. He felt his cheeks burn.

'And what have you learned about the Assamese mind so far?' Joy mama examined Ved.

'I can't tell,' Ved said. 'It seems to slide around corners before I can encounter it.'

'Ha!'

'You might like this bit,' said Ved, encouraged to read aloud. '"The media men beeline to the State to measure the fury of the red river, to gauge the intensity of the earth tremors or to carry back whatever inspires the sensational headlines ... Some others [come] just to have the thrills of a sojourn to another world. All of them ... go back without confronting the Assamese mind."'

Joy mama chuckled. 'I *like* you, Ved,' he said, as though the confession had been wrested from him. 'You're a student of human nature. Have some more whisky.'

'Thanks,' Ved said.

'I'm very fond of Ketu, you know, Ved,' Joy mama said. 'We've always been great friends. I do worry about her sometimes. What's to become of a person who lives alone? It's one thing for me, and even then, only in recent years. Otherwise, we were all here, my sister on and off given everything—and my older brother was here for a time, our parents before that.' He smiled, like a lion with a secret. 'I must say though, living alone is glorious, isn't it?'

'Yes,' Ved said. 'Although—'

Joy mama's eyes were sharp. 'You'd like a companion?'

Ved was about to say, 'I think I want to marry your niece,' when the door opened and Keteki came in.

Her uncle smiled. 'Come, Ketu,' he said, holding out a hand. Ved beamed, his blood full of whisky.

Keteki pulled up a cane stool. 'The good whisky?' she said, raising an eyebrow. 'You seem to have tamed my intractable uncle, Ved.' She grinned at him and took a glass from the tray.

'We've been discussing the Assamese mind, Ketu,' said her uncle.

Keteki rolled her eyes. 'Let me know what you conclude,' she said. 'Or don't bother. I have a funny relationship with Assam, Ved. I feel very Assamese when I'm outside, but on the edge of things when I'm here.' She shrugged and reached for the plate of snacks, taking a piece of what appeared to be deep fried bread. 'Tuku really knows how to fry things,' she observed.

'The boy is a gem,' said Joy mama.

'We're so lucky to have him in our family,' Keteki said. 'There's an amazing story about how he came to be here. As a baby, he was found in the train station in a basket. My other uncle was a government officer, and they took the baby to his office. Then he came to this house. We were very close when we were young. He's only about a year older than me.'

'You used to play together,' Joy mama said.

'At that time, the cook looked after Tuku,' Keteki went on. 'She was my mother's old nurse. Tuku and I spent all our time together when my parents and I were here. There was one game we had. Tuku made it up. We called it Bhex bodoli, which is like, transformation—how would you translate that?' She turned to her uncle.

He considered. 'The shape-shifting game,' he said.

Keteki nodded. 'We would point at something—a person or an object—and say it to each other, bhex bodoli. Quietly. And then the other person had to imagine what that thing magically turned into.' She laughed. 'After a while, we almost didn't have to say anything, we could just look at something and *see* it changing, together.'

Tipsy, Ved looked experimentally at different objects—an armchair, the bookcase, the standing lamp, to imagine them metamorphosing. Maybe the lampshade—

'Hang on,' he heard someone say a little too loudly, and realised it was him, but without being able to stop the second half of the sentence. 'Is that lampshade made of *skin*?'

Keteki eyed him, but Joy mama was indulgent. 'Yes, Ved, yes. Camel skin,' he said. 'My elder brother brought it in Khartoum.'

'Khartoum?' said Ved.

'Or was it Timbuktu?' mused the older man.

Ved gave up. 'So you said you spent a lot of time outside Assam,' he prompted Keteki.

'Boarding school,' she said.

'Right. So then, your parents—'

'It's such a long story, Ved,' Keteki said. She smiled at him, a smile of infinite understanding sought and accepted, a smile that told him that, in the entire world, only he knew what she thought and felt.

'Ah,' said Ved, not realising he'd spoken. He put his glass down on a coaster, imprecisely, smearing the table. 'Fuck. Ah, sorry.'

Joy mama rose. 'Leave that here, Ved. Don't worry, there's some wine with dinner. No need to give me any sort of look, Ketu,' he added over his shoulder. 'Let's eat, I'm famished.'

'Shall we?' Keteki got up too.

Shall we what, thought Ved as he followed her out. Get married, move in together, fuck each other's brains out? Everything was so unclear. In two days, he was supposed to leave Assam and go home via Bombay.

She hovered in the passage as though waiting for him to remember himself. He bumped into her. 'Sorry,' she said calmly. 'We're eating in the dining room.'

They went into a room with a long, polished teak table, and a candelabra on it. Keteki said something admiring to Tuku, who was leaving the room by a door on the far side. He smiled at her.

Joy mama was at the head of the table, and waved Ved to his left. 'We're eating a mixture of things. Traditional Assamese food and a few other dishes. Have some wine.'

'Well,' Ved was beginning.

'Best to fortify yourself,' said the older man. 'What if you have to encounter the Assamese mind before breakfast?'

'Only if he's very lucky,' said Keteki, making Ved choke. He took a sip of the wine, which was red and quite nice.

'Sorry, Ved?' said Joy mama.

'Nice wine,' Ved managed.

'I'm so glad. Now, first we have some mutton cutlets. Tuku makes them very well, though I shouldn't say it.'

Ved applied himself. The cutlets were delicious, finely minced with a hint of ginger and green chilli. He looked across at Keteki and saw her glance at her uncle, who was talking. Ved felt a lurch of envy, for in Keteki's look there was amusement, care, but most clearly love.

'And what do you think, Ved?'

'I—' Ved had been looking at Keteki, thinking his thoughts. Love: who budgeted for love? The kind of people who looked for it all the time didn't know what it was. 'Well, the cutlets. They're so good.'

Joy mama asked Tuku if there were more. 'Bade, he says he is ready to serve the next dishes, but he can bring you a cutlet along with the rice.'

'Hey, Tuku's really gone to so much trouble, nai?' said Keteki. 'I like the candles, it feels like a power cut.'

'It's a graceful light,' Joy mama said. 'You know, when we were young, there was electric light, but it was so much brighter. Yellow light. We still mostly have the old type of bulb in the house. Tuku has been putting in low energy bulbs in some places, but I can't tolerate them.'

'Can I tell him about the Everlasting Lucifer?' Keteki asked.

Joy mama chuckled. 'Sounds like me,' he said. 'An old devil. I remember the factory from my younger days, Ved.'

'The bulb lasts almost as long as a human life,' Keteki went on. 'But it isn't like those CFCs or whatever—'

'CFL,' murmured Ved.

'Whatever. Or the LEDs. LED?' She turned to him; her face seemed to have grown more luminous.

'Yes,' he said, too fervently. Both uncle and niece looked at him.

'It's like—not like *sun*light,' she explained to her uncle, 'but a sort of warm, soft, bright light. When I met Ved in Bombay, we put one of the bulbs in a socket and sat there looking out at the sea. It was so beautiful.'

Joy mama glanced at Ved. Yes, thought Ved, elated as well as embarrassed, I seduced your niece with a light bulb. That's the sort of man I am.

Instead, he said, 'They're developing another prototype, for larger spaces. Like schools, or—namghors.' He pronounced the new word carefully. 'It'll be like a fluorescent tube, but give the same kind of light as the Everlasting.'

Tuku appered in the background to remove the dishes. Keteki touched his wrist as he took away her plate, and he put his hand on her head for a moment.

'I sometimes wonder,' said Joy mama, 'if the human body is designed to cope with all these innovations. Artificial light, for example. We used to go to bed when it was dark.'

'I still feel like sleeping early in winter, when the days are so short,' murmured Keteki.

Tuku came in with a large dull golden thali and put it before Ved, who thanked him.

'This is the real Assamese food, Ved,' Joy mama said. The centre of the thali held a perfect mound of rice; small bowls surrounded it.

'It looks amazing,' Ved said. He ate a mouthful of delicious, gamey curry and rice, then a bit of mashed potato spiked with shards of green chilli. 'This potato is incredible,' he said.

'Aloo pitika,' Keteki said.

'And the curry?'

'Duck, Ved,' said Joy mama. 'It's a winter speciality.'

'There's a very annoying proverb,' Keteki said. 'About how the sleeping fox doesn't catch the duck. It's the kind of thing people say to you if you sleep late.'

Her uncle chuckled. 'We have a lot of proverbs,' he observed. 'Some are quite cryptic. For example,' and he said something in Assamese.

'Can you say it again more slowly?' Ved asked, concentrating.

'Xaatbhogiya maatit, xogoneu xo nakhai. Literally, on land that belongs to seven people, even a vulture doesn't eat a dead body.'

Ved gaped.

Keteki's uncle laughed. 'It describes a situation where there are too many interests and no one is likely to gain.'

'But it's not like people go round spouting fokora jujona the whole time,' Keteki said. 'That would be very corny.'

'They are sententious,' said her uncle. 'But they also delineate an idea of who we are. A sense of ourselves as a nation.'

'India?' said a confused Ved.

'The Assamese nation, Ved,' Joy mama said. 'We were a kingdom for six hundred years.'

'But, in a way, it's a construct,' Keteki said.

'The idea of Assam?'

Joy mama nodded. 'That is there, of course. Any search for the original people of a place is a kind of story. When the Ahoms came to this land, they called it their golden bowl. You must have seen the afternoon light on the countryside as you go further up—places like Sibsagar.'

Ved smiled. 'It is very beautiful.'

'There is something unearthly about this land,' Joy mama said.

'I felt that,' Ved admitted.

'I think you're overstating this,' Keteki said. Her tone was almost warning. 'Isn't it a bit of a cliché? Like people used to say until not so long ago that Assam was full of black magic and witchcraft or tantra or whatever.'

'But it is kind of magical, isn't it?' said Ved, slightly surprised to hear himself speak the words.

Keteki shrugged. 'What does that mean? Just because it's a beautiful place, and you don't understand the customs? That doesn't make it esoteric.'

Ved felt foggy. The light in the room seemed to have dimmed; maybe the voltage had dropped. 'But isn't it a bit esoteric? I mean, outsiders don't seem to understand it. And it seems to me that the most important values are assumed, not stated. Is that fair?'

'Yes, but—'

Ved had a moment of drunken clarity. The aureoles of the candles seemed to go fuzzy as he said, 'But if it was esoteric, you wouldn't tell me, would you?'

Joy mama laughed.

'Don't you think, when things are put into words, they lose some of their basic *essence*?' Keteki said. She was looking at Ved intently, and he melted.

'Tantra,' said Joy mama.

'What is tantra, actually?' asked Ved.

Joy mama began to explain something, but other than the words 'technical' and 'weaving', Ved was able to retain nothing. All he could focus on was candlelight glinting off the handsome old man's spectacles and off the wine glasses. Ved put down his fork. 'It's absolutely dlishious,' he heard himself declare as Tuku came in with a further tray.

'Just try the paex,' Joy mama urged. 'Rice pudding, Ved, very light.' Tuku put a bowl in front of Ved.

'Your uncle smazing,' said Ved to Keteki as they lurched down the corridor some time later.

A while after that, he woke in bed in his room. He was still drunk, and his head now hurt. After a moment, he realised that he and Keteki were wrapped in each other's arms like slumbering kittens. She was in pyjamas; he wore a T-shirt and boxers. He sighed, put his head back on the pillow, tucked his chin over the warm crown of her head and closed his eyes.

10

Inside out

'UGH,' KETEKI SAID. 'I think I have a hangover. Why …' She laughed into Ved's neck. They were still clothed, still entangled. He smelled her hair, but stayed still. A cool sunlight came in under the orange curtains.

'We drank too much,' said Ved. He rubbed his eyes.

'What possessed us to drink that mead?' Keteki wondered. 'That bottle's been there God knows how long. I'm getting some water. Do you want anything?' She disentangled herself and stumbled up.

A little later, Ved looked over to see her in the armchair, intent on her phone. 'Are you up now?' he asked.

'Water,' she said, pointing at the bedside table. Ved raised himself on an elbow, poured a glass and drank it. 'Maybe I should brush my teeth,' he said, eyeing her.

'I don't think it's time yet,' Keteki said. She got back into bed, wrapped an arm and a leg around him under and over the covers, and was asleep again. Her body emanated a steady glow that warmed Ved. Time passed. There were noises, perhaps from the side of the house. The light under the curtain became orange.

Keteki got up and went out. She returned some time later, wearing jeans and a hoodie, and handed Ved a cup of tea. Tuku came in, gave her another cup, and went out, leaving the door half ajar. Keteki sat in the armchair, drinking her tea. She seemed to be thinking. Ved was aware of her doing it, present to witness it in a way he was rarely present for anything. He felt she'd been there forever, or perhaps he had.

A thought came to him. 'Your uncle is so great,' he said. He sat up, sipped his tea. 'He's so interesting. That conversation. I don't remember all of it.' He rubbed his face. 'Is he always like that?'

Keteki curled further in the chair, like the inhabitant of a nautilus. 'He loves to talk,' she said. 'We all do. But he's so good at it.' She grinned, and dangled her legs over the side of the chair.

'And your parents, remind me,' Ved said.

Her smile faded. 'Not on a hangover, Ved.'

'Okay, sorry.' He lay down again and regarded her under his lashes. Was there any possibility of going back to bed in earnest? What about sex? On the other hand, sleeping entangled with her was better than a lot of things.

She looked up and smiled. 'Let's go and find the magic talking uncle,' she said.

Ved laughed and got up.

Joy mama was outside, somehow managing to look manly in a cardigan. 'Tuku!' he called when he saw them. 'Morning, morning, Ved. How did you sleep?'

'I think I overslept. I'm sorry,' Ved said.

'Not at all. Sit down. Tea? Coffee?'

'Coffee please.'

'The two of you look slightly the worse for wear,' observed Joy mama.

Ved sat down gingerly on a cane chair. Keteki folded herself into another and put up her hood.

Joy mama put down his newspaper and took off his glasses. 'Ved, it's winter,' he said, 'so you won't see the number of birds in the garden that we have in summer. The kuli—the cuckoo. Even white cranes. We call them bogoli. They are very funny looking birds, they roost in that tree over there. You can't imagine how ungainly they look.'

Keteki chuckled. 'They jump on a branch and it groans,' she said, laughing harder, apparently, than she'd intended. 'Ow,' she muttered, and rubbed her forehead.

Tuku appeared with coffee, some cut fruit, toast and omelettes. Keteki put some fruit on her plate, looked at it and suddenly got up. 'I'll just …' she said, and walked off, a thin figure in her hoodie and pyjamas.

'My niece,' observed Joy mama.

Ved smiled at him. 'I think she's great,' he said.

The other man smiled, then frowned. 'Ketu has had quite a strange upbringing. My sister and my brother-in-law didn't really get along, led quite an irregular life. Keteki was sent to school when she was very young, a long way away. At an age when a child should be put to sleep by her parents, she was in a dormitory somewhere surrounded by strangers. Although there were reasons for that.'

'Put to sleep?' said Ved.

Joy mama gave him an odd look. 'Children here sleep with their parents until they are quite old, maybe six or seven. Or someone will lie with them until they are asleep, you know.'

'I didn't know that,' Ved said. He felt a blurring of despair at the idea of the person he might have been, cuddled into slumber from babyhood.

Joy mama sighed, rubbed the tips of his fingers together and stared into the garden. Eventually, he roused himself. 'Ved, what will you have? More toast? Coffee?'

When Ved returned to his room, he found Keteki asleep in the bed. He hurried to shower and dry himself, then got in with her. They slept into the afternoon. When one moved, the other would wait before regrouping into an embrace of arms and legs, cheek on chest or shoulder.

A little after dusk, Keteki, who was sleeping near the window, put her right leg over Ved's. The leg tightened, and she ground herself vaguely against his hip bone. He waited, tense. She reached up, eyes still closed, and kissed his cheek. Tentatively, she put her lips to his. Ved put his tongue in her warm mouth, pulled her close, and stroked the curve where her buttocks met her legs under the thin cotton. She had her arms around his neck, one hand on his nape. He put a hand under her T-shirt, felt her breathe as he cupped a breast, rubbed the nipple with the flat of his hand, the tips of his fingers. She sat up, eyes still half-closed, and pulled off her top. Ved kneeled over her, kissing and sucking her nipples. They still tasted like smoky tea, salted meat or basic goodness. He took off his T-shirt. Keteki reached into his waistband. When she held his cock, he whimpered. 'The door,' he said. He jumped up and went to it.

'A bolt at the top,' Keteki said. She'd pulled off her pyjamas by the time he reached the bed. He squirmed out of his boxers and kneeled over her. She helped him in and he moved, bending down to kiss her. She lifted her hips; the curtain moved with a cool breeze; it was raining outside. Ved came suddenly and hugely and, smiling, kept kissing Keteki, who stroked his back. After a moment, he rolled off her and took her in his arms. They slept for a bit. 'Did you come?' he asked.

The rain was soft but steady outside.

'No,' she said.

'I thought so … I'm sorry,' he mumbled.

She reached up to kiss his cheek, and fell asleep on his chest.

A while later, he became aware of Keteki being awake, or rather not being in his dream. He opened his eyes. 'What if I get turned on again?' he asked.

She smiled. 'I think it's time to get up,' she said.

He watched her sit upright, locate her clothes, her long, honey-coloured body, shoulders bony and hips full. She was uncoordinated after sleeping and stumbled as she searched for something. Finally she said, 'Ved, where's my T-shirt?'

It was under his leg.

She put it on and smiled at him. 'I'm going to take a bath in my room. Your geyser's on. Come out whenever you're ready.'

That night, when they went to bed, he held her. They were facing each other.

'Your uncle,' Ved says. 'I think he worries about you.'

'Hm,' said Keteki, into his neck.

'He really cares about you.'

'He loves me,' she said, tenderness in her voice mingled with pain.

'What do you want to do?' Ved said. 'What's your plan?'

Keteki's voice was sleepy. 'Plan?'

'I'd love to be involved,' Ved said. 'In the future. Your future. I mean, I want to be a part of it.'

Keteki was silent.

'What do you think?' Ved asked. He put his nose in her hair. Her head smelled extraordinary, like a baby's.

'Ved,' she said, 'you know, the *future* ... I don't think I really believe in the future.'

She wriggled out of his hold, but her arm remained around him. She gazed over his shoulder.

'Okay,' Ved said. 'But what does that actually mean? You've done normal human things, you got a degree, you've acted as though you did believe in a future, otherwise ...'

'Otherwise I would still be in this house, chasing the cats up the corridor at night, and reading my uncle's books about yoga, yes,' Keteki said. She took away her arm and stared at the ceiling. 'Meditating and waiting to see my own face in the sky.'

'Your what?'

She smiled. 'It's a thing that happens, apparently, at a certain stage. But you're not supposed to get distracted by it.'

Ved waited.

She sighed and turned to him again. 'It's true,' she said. 'I do normal things, or I have. But I don't really— What I'm saying, maybe, is that it makes more sense for me to behave as though the future didn't exist.' Her voice was soft but clear.

'Is that nihilism?' Ved said. 'Or living in the present?'

'It's so *tedious*, isn't it, when people talk about living in the present,' Keteki said. He felt the laugh shake her.

'I don't know,' Ved said.

'Why are you doing this,' Keteki complained. 'I didn't think you were like this.'

Ved considered. He still had a hand on her thigh. For once, he felt adult; he was barely even thinking of the usual manipulations or manoeuvres. 'Maybe,' he said, 'maybe it's just time to live, instead of trying to avoid things.'

Keteki turned to him. Her mouth was against his throat. He was aware of her looking at the window, although the curtain was closed, and it was dark outside. He heard footsteps somewhere, and felt her absence. 'Mm,' she said quietly. 'I can understand that.' A little later she licked his collarbone. Then, at more length than in the afternoon, they fucked. She came.

11

Dhudor Ali

VED WOKE TO find a voicemail from a distraught-sounding Rajen. There had been a big fire at the factory. Although no one had been hurt, the damage was severe.

An hour and a half later, a taxi was waiting outside the door for Ved.

'See you tomorrow evening,' he said to Keteki and her uncle. He saw them in the rear-view mirror, Joy mama tall and stocky, Keteki next to him. She looked slender, appearing almost to dematerialise as they pulled out of the gate.

They drove through town with the windows open, cold air and traffic fumes mingling with the remnants of the winter mist. The winter sun was rarefied: they drove through it as through a new element.

Ved looked out of the window. The buildings by the highway were in different stages of being demolished, the fronts broken and bare. Around them, people swept up the detritus. They were getting ready to rebuild fifty yards further from the new, widened highway. Their lives seemed as though opened up by a surgery left abandoned, a natural disaster they hadn't yet noticed. The journey was long, and Ved kept wanting to text Keteki, but not doing it. He'd only just seen her, and he'd be back tomorrow. Why was he so anxious? The cold in his knuckles, nose, ears and ankles brought back unwanted memories of those first months in England. Six-year-old Ved, in his grey Woolworths coat with fake fur on the hood; cross-country afternoons at school, where the kids, wearing shorts, T-shirts and stupid cotton pumps, would plod along a cold muddy field while teachers in jeans, coats and wellies followed. One particular moment of shame: everyone else in the crocodile had crossed a small, freezing stream; only Ved, frozen in every sense, stalled like a horse in front of the running water. He could imagine how cold the water would be, how ridiculous he'd look when he fell in. 'Come on!' snapped the teacher. 'It's very easy.'

Ved called Rajen as he neared the factory, but the big man said, 'Listen, Ved, I'm tied up today with the police, and I have to talk to Mr Ganesh after that. Let's meet in the morning.'

Ganesh called Ved later in the evening, after Ved had ordered and eaten room-service dinner and a beer in his hotel room.

'The police are questioning all the workers, but we don't want the usual intimidation to come into play,' he said.

'What could have happened?' Ved asked.

'The investigation has started, let's wait a few days to see what comes to light,' the older man said quietly.

'But the launch?' Ved asked.

'Yes,' Ganesh said. 'We are nearly ready to send you the advertisement, it's very good I think. And of course production in Chennai is going fine. So, let's see.'

Ved thought. 'Okay,' he said. 'Maybe a small delay won't be the end of the world.'

But in the morning, walking around the site with Rajen, he said, 'Shit.' Then, 'Sorry.'

Rajen sighed. 'Shit more or less hits the nail on the head, Ved. We don't know much yet. But it seems to have begun inside, though we're not sure when. Once the fire was hotter, of course the packed bulbs started exploding. Sunday is the one day there's no night shift, and this isn't a residential area, so no one reported anything.'

Ved looked back at the charred building.

'The *strangest* thing,' Rajen said, is that we have the CCTV footage.' He turned to Ved, and his face was helpless. 'But there's no sign of anyone coming or going for hours before the flame began.'

Ved left in the afternoon. It was already dark.

Rajen said a hurried farewell. 'Ved, I'm telling him to take you by Dhudor Ali, the old road. It's winding and narrow, but there's going to be a bandh tomorrow, and unrest might start tonight. Nothing major, don't worry. Some of the local groups are protesting for reservation, ST status. They'll stop cars, create trouble if they see people on the roads.'

The car pulled out. Before long, they were on Dhudor Ali. Ved remembered Joy mama talking about the road, built by the Dhuds, an unofficial group of sixteenth-century slackers who smoked opium and took a lot of naps until one of the Ahom kings took exception to their lifestyle and set them to work building a road of a hundred miles through upper Assam. They had managed to do even this inordinately slowly.

Ved wondered if the Dhuds had somehow soaked the road in slowness, a slowness that would never leave it. Driving on Dhudor Ali in the evening was a syrupy descent into a dream, the kind of dream in which you decide to move your arm and, centuries later, see it move, the kind of dream in which you say to yourself, this dream is very funny, but it's just a dream, I am dreaming.

Bijoy, the driver, laboured along Dhudor Ali, which was more a miraculous necklace of potholes than a modern tarmac road. He had to drive more or less continually in second gear, and very soon put on a playlist of what sounded like sweet Sixties pop songs in Assamese. Ved tried to stop checking his phone every two minutes to see if Keteki had replied to his text letting her know he'd be back in time for dinner. He tried to relax into the mood of unrelentingly sweet melancholy and stared at the odometer. Every half hour or so, they managed a few more kilometres.

'Who is this singer?' he asked Bijoy.

'One of our most popular singers, sir. Old time. Jayanta Hazarika.'

The little roadside shops were all shuttered to comply with the bandh. Once in a while, they saw a ghostly cyclist in white; otherwise, the road was nearly empty.

It was after ten when they arrived at the white-painted wooden gate in Choladhara. Ved tipped Bijoy hugely and rang the bell.

Joy mama opened the door. Ved absorbed the other man's emotion of embarrassment without realising it. 'Ved,' he said heavily. 'Come in, come in. You've had a long journey. Let's have a drink.'

When Ved got to the drawing room, the standard lamp with the odd skin-lampshade was lit, casting a warm glow.

But Joy mama looked depressed. 'Whisky, Ved?' he suggested, waving at the armchairs near the French doors. On the table was a tray with the bottle, some water and two glasses.

'I—' said Ved. There was a long pause, as a moth battered itself against the bulb in the standard lamp. Finally Ved said, 'Keteki's not here? When did she leave?'

'In the morning,' Joy mama said. 'Not that long after you.'

'She's gone back to Guwahati,' Ved said. He would see her there.

'Actually, Ved, I don't think so. Maybe Delhi. She said she had some work. I feel bad about this, you know. Won't you sit down?'

The whisky he handed Ved was the smoky malt they'd drunk a couple of days earlier. Now it tasted of rot and meths.

Ved looked at Joy mama. The other man was silent, wholly present, his eyes round and dark. Ved said, 'I can't quite believe …'

Joy mama poured him more whisky. 'Ved,' he said, 'go and have a wash, get changed. We'll eat as soon as you're ready.'

Ved nodded, blinked, swallowed and got up, taking his glass with him. 'Thanks,' he said.

12

Barsati

JANUARY IN DELHI: either end of the day, the air was smoky, polluted. 'But I like winter here,' Keteki said. 'Everything feels calmer.' She turned to Sumit, who lay next to her on the mattress in Priya and Sunando's terrace room. 'Sumit, don't sleep here. I think that would be a bit much.'

'Do you want to come back to Gulmohar Park with me?' He was staying with a friend, and the conference he'd come for had ended that evening. 'We could go to Sarojini Nagar tomorrow and look at all that shit you like so much.' He laughed, more like a naughty child than an assistant professor of economics.

'It's not shit,' Keteki said mildly. 'Or, well, it is, but you don't understand.' She took out her phone. 'See. It's not the individual things. It's the aggregate. Look at the pattern. One of these huge foam bras is not that interesting. But when you look at them arranged like columns—'

'I get it, I get it. So come with me now, and we can walk round in the morning while you take photographs.'

Keteki yawned. 'I would have loved to, Sumit. But all my stuff is here.' She looked at him, hoping he'd just go.

Maybe she shouldn't have picked up when he called this afternoon. She'd come here for a few days to escape, as well as for a few work things, like meeting the printer a friend had recommended whose work was excellent.

Sumit lit the second half of a joint.

'Don't smoke inside,' Keteki protested.

'Don't be uptight, man.' He finished getting dressed, propped the joint on the coffee table next to her sofa bed, picked up the used condom and shoved it back in its wrapping. 'What do I do with this?'

'Take it with you,' Keteki invited. 'Give it to your cabbie as a tip.'

Sumit laughed. 'That sounds like a nice way to end up murdered next to the Ring Road.' He looked around. 'Stuff? All you have is a backpack.' He took a long toke and squinted.

'It's good not to get weighed down.'

'What about that guy, the British one?' Sumit remembered. 'He seemed keen.'

Keteki squirmed. 'It's not like that,' she said. 'He was going to be in Assam for work anyway. I took him to my uncle's house in Jorhat, they got on.'

'Oh, so you didn't ditch him?' But Sumit's phone had begun to buzz. The taxi. 'Haan bhaiya, aa raha hun,' he said. 'See you back in Guwahati, Keteki.' They hugged and he left. Keteki turned out the light and slept.

Some time later, when sunlight came through the curtain, she got up and yawned. Then said, 'Oh, fuck.'

There was a large rusty stain on the sheet. She pulled it off the mattress: hardly a spot there. But she'd have to wash the sheet. Her back ached. She needed to find a tampon, get to the bathroom, get some detergent, deal with the sheet, tell

Priya. She wiped herself with some tissue and started to go down the stairs. On the landing, she bumped into Sunando.

'Sorry! Good morning. Sunando, is Priya here?'

'No, she had a meeting,' her host said quietly. He was mild-mannered, his hair receding and cropped close; she'd known him and Priya since her early twenties, when she and a group of other friends used their house as an informal hostel when in Delhi. 'Can I help?'

'Nothing, nothing,' said Keteki. 'I spilled something. On the mattress. I need to clean it.'

'Don't worry, let me go take a look,' Sunando said.

'No!'

He stopped. 'No?'

'I got my period,' Keteki said. 'There's some blood on the sheet.' She was surprised at how embarrassed she was.

'Oh! That's okay. I'll put it in the machine. Do you need a painkiller?'

'Do you have one?'

'I think Sumi has a stash of Meftal somewhere. I'll look. Were you about to take a bath? I'll ask Shefali to change the sheet, and maybe we can have some coffee on the terrace in about half an hour, unless you're going out?'

When she returned, warm and clothed, he was sitting on a low chair near the coffee table, just under the extending roof. He and Priya used the terrace room as a study when it wasn't occupied by one of their many guests.

Keteki sat on the other side, on a cane stool. 'Barsatis are one of the best things about Delhi,' she said. 'I like being outside it. From here, it feels so—'

Sunando looked back at the little structure, really just a shack. He laughed. 'Khatara?' he suggested.

'Provisional,' she said. 'Like the bamboo huts we have at home. Light, and not too much stuff in them.' She looked out at the sky, the clouds and mist, the other roofs of the city. 'Do you think the beginning of the world looked like this?' she asked. 'When things were just being filled in.'

Sunando handed her a cup of coffee. 'Maybe,' he said. 'Just akash, you mean?'

Keteki smiled. 'You'd get on with my uncle,' she said.

'The one who studied in Paris?'

'And who does yoga, like you. He was even vegetarian for a while. In Assam, that's virtually like performing the dark rites or something.'

Sunando chuckled. 'I'd like to meet him.'

It began to rain softly, smudging out the concrete world.

'He doesn't really fit in,' Keteki said. 'That's probably why I feel so at home with him. I always feel more connected to Assam when I'm away.' She felt ungrounded, a little light-headed, and was aware of her body working hard.

'It's funny, isn't it,' Sunando said. He leaned back in his chair, and she thought of all the times she'd seen him at parties, a joint in his hand. 'The more things seem fixed, the more one has the urge to run off. I do too, you know.' He looked at Keteki, and sipped his coffee. 'Not a marital crisis or anything, though I doubt there's any marriage worth the name that hasn't had a few crises. But when I was younger, I put my energy into building things. Making a system. I had a vision of how life should be.' He laughed, his shoulders hunched. 'So pompous. Things kept happening, a child, work, some measure of success and, suddenly, before the point where we could even relax, the decline had already begun.' He laughed again, showing gently ivoried teeth.

The rain fell harder. Keteki thought of all the places it must touch: slums, the sludgy Yamuna, the terraces of the rich, the gardens of government officers, shopping malls, mouldy air conditioners.

'When I was quite young,' she said, 'I assumed that when I grew up I would be some sort of sannyasin. I never really told anyone this. It must sound very silly.'

Sunando smiled. 'Not necessarily. You saw yourself in orange?'

'I remember looking at my parents one evening, a rare evening when we were all at home, and they were reading and listening to music, not shouting at each other or out or in their separate rooms,' Keteki said. 'I thought, One day I'll have to leave them—leave everything, and go away alone. I thought about how sad they'd be, and that I mustn't tell them, I must protect them from it.' She shrugged. 'In the end, I did go away, but to boarding school, and it was more or less their idea. And now, this transient life.'

'There must be something that anchors you,' Sunando said. 'Work?'

'Yes and no.' She thought of Ved. 'You know, my childhood wasn't so easy. I was probably oversensitive and there were some things—family problems. I was sent away, my mother's oldest brother became estranged from the rest of the family, my parents divorced, which was more or less unheard of at the time in Assam. Now, I see in myself this reluctance to get involved with anything seriously. There's a fear of losing myself. It's simpler to keep a distance.' She put down the cup on the table. The sky had darkened.

'Sometimes we just have to be gentle with ourselves,' Sunando said.

Keteki felt like crying. 'That sounds like a dangerous habit to get into,' she managed.

'Before Sumi went away to study, she had this period—you know she dropped out of LSR, she had a relationship that didn't go well, a lot of things became difficult for her. I don't think we saw so much of you during this time.'

'I didn't know,' Keteki said. 'How are things now?'

'She's so much happier. Something that really helped was going off for this yoga course in the mountains. It's a teacher training, but there seem to be a lot of people who just go to reset themselves in some way,' Sunando said. 'I'm not really sure what it was, maybe the routine or the break from everything in Delhi, you know, too much familiarity, too many of the same people and places. But she was different after that. Maybe you should try it. Priya can give you the details when she's home.'

There was lightning, then a clap of thunder. The rain spat.

'We should close the doors,' Sunando said. They carried in the furniture. Sunando put on a lamp, half drew the curtains over the glass. The room had changed; it was warm and interior.

'I'll go down and see about lunch, deal with some emails,' he said. 'Let me know if you need anything.' He smiled at her and went out.

13

The Old Masters

EARLY MORNING IN the ashram. Keteki sat on the steps to the garden, sipping her milky tea and watching the river dance and the mountains rise green, white and grey into the sky, violet and orange. Across the river was a small village; behind the ashram, another, slightly larger one, which had hotels that served pakoras and tea, and shops that sold chocolate, cigarettes and hair oil. But it was all unreal, as they'd learned; not that this was much of a surprise.

Every spiritual master apparently had a brief summary of his teaching. Shankaracharya said: Brahman is real; the world is unreal; Brahman and atman are the same.

Mia, a Californian girl, touched Keteki's elbow. 'So remind me, Brahman is like …'

'The thing that makes everything happen. Not makes,' Keteki qualified. 'It doesn't do anything. But it underlies everything.'

'And it's invisible?'

'Yes, and we're all part of it. There's no difference between Brahman and the individual soul.' Keteki looked through the wrought-iron gate to the river bank. A monitor lizard was hanging off the small tree outside the gate, showing off.

'But,' Mia persisted, 'I don't get it. Brahman created the world? Why?'

'There's no explanation.' Keteki shrugged, and watched a butterfly dance in the sun. 'For fun? It was bored?'

As they were laughing, the bell rang for asana class. While the other girl went to get changed, Keteki remained where she was. The Ganga rushed, the lizard clung to its tree, the sun shone. The scene was impossibly pretty, an Impressionist painting become three-dimensional, all light and brightness. In comparison, Keteki's own life, especially the earlier part, which she'd spent a lot of time thinking about during her first fortnight in the ashram, seemed dark and full of frightening-looking faces rendered in subdued earth pigments: yellow ochre, Venetian red, burnt umber. The Old Masters, she thought, and remembered, with a pain in her belly, the little darkened room in Jorhat where she used to be put to sleep as a young child.

'And the Gita tells us to treat whatever takes place as prasad, holy food—to welcome everything that happens. Why might that be?'

Lev, the Israeli boy, put up his hand. 'Because we don't have a choice?'

Some tired laughter.

'It's true, we have no choice,' said the teacher. 'But that's not the full reason.'

Juanita, the Spanish girl from Keteki's dormitory, put up her hand. 'Because it's a result of our past karma?'

The Gita teacher nodded. He was a slender man with glasses and a ponytail. 'Which type of karma?'

'The older one ... from previous lives,' someone else said.

'Sanchita karma, yes. But what is the name for the things we choose to work through in a specific life?'

Keteki put up her hand, mainly so that the class would move on. 'Prarabdha karma,' she said. She looked out of the window, across to the opposite bank of the river, and saw a Garhwali woman, beautiful in embroidered blouse and skirt, weighed down under a bundle of firewood.

'There's a real sense in which,' the teacher was saying, 'you must all have done a lot of good things in previous lives to be here now, on the banks of the Ganga, ready to become,' he smiled, 'jnanis, enlightened people.'

In the evening after dinner, Keteki went to the garden. She saw the Gita teacher sitting on a bench. 'May I join you?' she asked.

'Please,' he said.

'I was wondering ...' Keteki said.

He looked at her.

'Have you ever met a jnani?'

'My teacher. You should hear his lectures on the Gita. He's extraordinary.'

'Do you think he's enlightened?'

The Gita teacher smiled. 'I asked him once. He said, "They say it takes a jnani to recognise a jnani. So when you become a jnani, you will be able to tell if I am one or not." But I think he is,' he added. 'He's so calm.'

'You seem calm too,' Keteki said.

The teacher exhaled. 'I tried everything,' he said. 'Yoga, running, ayahuasca, tantra, Prozac, beta blockers.'

Keteki listened, her head tilted to one side. 'What did you do before this? Your work?' she asked.

'I was a philosophy professor.'

'Really?' she laughed.

'Vedanta is the only thing that worked for me. It doesn't try to prove what it asserts. But it made sense to me.'

Keteki hesitated. 'And before that,' she began to ask, but another student appeared.

'Can I join you?' he asked.

'Please,' said the Gita teacher. More and more students filtered into the garden; the river, it seemed, grew even louder in the dark.

The next afternoon, Keteki went for a walk and tea across the footbridge with Pauline, an American girl from her dormitory.

They sipped the tea, and munched cashew-nut cookies, sitting on a wooden bench next to the tea stall and looking at the river, and to the right the Himalayas, blue, green and white, reaching into the sky.

'This view …' Keteki said.

'It's ridiculous,' said the other girl cheerfully.

Keteki smiled; she liked Pauline's calm and her decisiveness, her large blue eyes and thick hair.

'I've started thinking about what I'm going to do after I get home,' Pauline said. She'd been working in marketing in New York, but was thinking of moving back to Northern California to teach. 'Leaving the big city feels like a sort of failure. But I'm tired. I want to see the ocean.'

Keteki nodded. 'That makes sense.'

'What's next for you?'

Keteki looked across the river at the candy-coloured ashram. 'I do these freelance projects, mostly curation, but sometimes related things, like book design. It's weird, because I didn't really train in design, I studied history of art.' She shrugged. 'Sometimes I work a lot and earn quite a bit, sometimes I don't work for a little while. I just keep letting things happen.'

'That sounds very zen,' Pauline said. 'Hey, should we go back to change in time for asana class?'

As they were walking up to the bridge, Keteki said, 'I keep thinking about working with the textiles from the northeast. There are amazing handloom fabrics from different communities in all the states—women used to weave them at home.'

'That sounds so interesting. Would you be documenting it?'

A boy passed them, walking in the other direction. He led a pretty red bullock, who blinked eyes fringed with long lashes.

'I was thinking of making simple clothes—using those textiles in a way that makes them into everyday clothing. In a way, that's appropriating them, but in another way, I think it would transmit something about that tribe, that community. I'm still just thinking about it, I guess.'

The bridge creaked, and swayed in the wind.

In the asana class, they worked on the headstand. Keteki still hadn't managed one; she could pull in her knees and begin to straighten her legs, but so fast that they would start wobbling.

Erin, the Australian assistant, came to help. 'Hey. Slow down, slow down.'

Keteki sat up and gave her a frustrated grin.

'What's the hurry?' Erin asked. 'You need to stop thinking about where you're trying to go, and feel where you are.'

'Partner work,' called the teacher.

'Ready?' said Iago, who was next to Keteki. 'You go first.'

She made a tripod with her arms, stood on tiptoes and inched towards her shoulders. Her feet came off the ground, and she hugged her knees into her abdomen. One leg straightened, then the other. Iago grabbed her ankles.

'Wait,' Keteki said. 'I—'

'You're not stable enough,' Iago said. He was her friend; she liked his steadiness and warmth.

'But I—no, don't. I don't want to.' It was difficult to explain while upside down. She didn't want him to steady her; she wanted to tremble into steadiness on her own.

'You need to straighten out.' Iago, six-foot-something and about three times Keteki's weight, pulled her up by the ankles. Her elbows lifted from the floor.

'No! Stop it, don't! I don't *want* you to.'

She was unsure when her voice rose and the moment turned, but abruptly other people were looking. Keteki, red with shame, was put down. She rested her forehead on the floor, then lifted her face, wet with tears.

Iago looked shaken. 'I was just helping,' he said.

Keteki sat up. 'But I didn't want it,' she said, and swallowed the rest.

In the dormitory, alone, she cried extravagantly, her shoulders heaving.

'Are you okay?' Pauline asked. Class wasn't over, but she'd come to use the bathroom.

'I just,' Keteki began. 'When I was younger—' But she didn't want to say it. 'I'm fine,' she said.

'I don't think Santiago meant to upset you,' Pauline said. 'I think he's a little upset himself now.'

'I know,' Keteki said. Why was she so disturbed? But she knew, and the reason made her feel defeated. After all these years, unbidden, it kept coming back, the little bedroom in Jorhat and her adored eldest uncle, Sandeep mama, coming in to lie with her till she slept. He'd been clear about one thing: if she told anyone, something very bad would happen.

She wiped her face. For some reason, the quiet of the ashram had brought back this memory, a canvas in dark colours, a man with a handsome, sometimes cruel face. Keteki had spent the first two weeks of the training bursting into tears randomly. She checked her phone now, noted the lack of messages from Ved, and thought dryly of her propensity for drama, or natok, when there was none.

In Gita class, they had learned that they too were nothing but unqualified bliss at the core. There was nothing to do, nothing to lose or gain. She believed this instinctively. Nothing about it was surprising. And yet, the wounds of the past remained.

In the evening satsang, she sat behind the tall Spaniard and gave him a bear hug, an apology he accepted without turning.

14

The story of Cupid and Psyche: Part I

THE PORTERS' LODGE was busy with returning alumni. Ahead of him, Ved spotted a girl he recognised. 'Hey,' he said, and smiled.

She looked him up and down and turned away. Ved gawped. He managed to dredge out her name: Christine Mo. They had been in the same year. Surely she had a dim memory of Ved's existence?

'Hello sir,' said the Head Porter. 'Here for the Annual Gathering?'

'Yup,' said Ved. 'Ved, V. 1996.'

'Right,' said the porter, opening an enormous ledger filled with passport photos. 'Let's see who you used to be.'

'Mario!' Ved approached the steward.

'Welcome back! Great to see you,' said Mario with a wide grin. He shoved a glass of champagne into Ved's hand. Behind Ved, the next person in line said, 'Mario! How are you?'

'Welcome back,' said the steward, with the same rictus. 'Great to see you!'

Ved turned. 'Hey, Leela Gosh,' he said.

'Oh, hi, Ved.' As ever, she broke the unspoken code by pronouncing his name properly.

'You cut your hair,' Ved said. Leela Ghosh, it'd been years since he'd seen her. She didn't look bad at all.

'Yes, I'm a lesbian now,' she said, staring into the distance.

'*Really?*' said Ved.

'No, but that's the kind of thing you'd probably think.' She looked up at him.

'There's no need to be aggressive,' Ved said. 'The glasses, the hair, they suit you, actually.'

'Yeah, thanks.'

'Hey man!' It was Nat, thumping Ved between the shoulder blades. 'Looking good.'

'Looking like everyone else here,' Ved said. When had wearing a suit but not wearing a tie turned into the I'm-sharp-but-not-boring uniform? Where did it leave people's necks, he wondered, then thought that was something Keteki might say, and felt sad. He breathed in the cool evening air and looked around Nevile's Court. The tall Malaysian girl from earlier was there, in a long dress with a thigh-high split. She looked pleased with life. Ved turned away, feeling inadequate. Under the suit, he was eighteen again.

But Nat was there, laughing and joking, and soon lots of others. Even Leela dropped her guard for a moment to smile at Ved. They were talking to Childe, a.k.a. Roland Thompson, a soft-faced guy who'd made the mistake of admitting at the interview that he'd been named after the Browning poem 'Childe Roland to the Dark Tower came'.

'I'm feeling good about myself,' Childe was saying. He was one of the few men who'd bothered to wear a tie, albeit a slightly horrible one, no doubt given to him by one of his offspring. 'I thought Stephenson might have more children than me, but I win! He's only got three.'

'How many do you have?' Ved asked.

Childe had married his girlfriend from school and had managed to get through college, as far as Ved knew, without shagging anyone else.

'Six,' said Childe calmly.

'Fuck, really?' said Ved. 'Isn't having kids super expensive though?'

'Economies of scale,' Childe said. 'Anyway, I bet you can afford it, Ved. I heard you've made a bob or two.'

'I don't know if I want kids,' Ved said.

'What do you do again?' Childe asked.

One of Mario's minions came round to fill up their glasses. Ved began to feel tipsy and socially capable, like all those years ago when alcohol first hit his system.

'Venture capital,' he said. 'Investing in businesses, advising them how to run.'

'Oh really? Is that the one where you buy a company and sack loads of people?'

'No, not at all,' Ved said. 'Well, look, sometimes there is some rationalisation. But there are some really cool projects. Like, in November last year I went out to India to this light bulb manufacturer—'

'Why,' interrupted Leela, 'do people feel the need to say *out* to India? Or *out* to France? It doesn't even serve any grammatical purpose. It's just a desperately provincial hangover of Europe.'

Childe and Ved regarded her with amusement and admiration, as they may have twenty years earlier. 'I suppose that's true,' said Childe, in his slow, calm way. 'There isn't any need to say that, "out to India". I wonder why we do.'

'Leela's a lesbian now,' said drunk Ved.

'Oh really?' said Childe politely. Nat rolled his eyes at Ved.

'No,' said Leela. 'That's just what Ved thinks about women with short hair because he's an oaf.'

'Do you happen to know the etymology of that word?' Ved was beginning, when the gong sounded.

The end of March: it was still light outside when the meal began. Ved was two places down from Nat. Childe was on Ved's right, Leela on his left. Candlelight glinted on silver, and Ved and Leela squabbled drunkenly throughout dinner. At one point, Ved smiled at their former director of studies and said hello. Rupert Foster looked blankly at him. 'Ved Ved,' said Ved. 'I, er, you—'

The older man had splendid wavy white hair, sparkling blue eyes, etc. He gave Ved a sceptical look. '*Ru*pert,' said Leela reproachfully. 'You remember Ved.' But Professor Foster didn't. Wow, thought Ved. I've been edited out of my own life.

'What's your problem?' Ved found himself saying to Leela halfway through his game terrine.

'I don't have a problem,' Leela said. 'Unlike you.'

Ved remembered her as mousy yet intense. They'd become friendly only in their final term. They would walk to the University Library together, though sometimes he avoided her at tea time so he could sit alone in the cafeteria, consuming a cheese scone the size of his head while staring at women from other colleges.

'What's wrong with you all?' he said, as they stood drinking port after dinner. 'Women. Why do you feel the need to take men apart?'

Leela stopped eviscerating Ved for a second and put her head to one side. 'What's up with you?' she asked.

'This woman,' Ved said. 'Beautiful, intelligent, sparky. I had a chance. But I fucked up, I don't even know how.'

At the end of a much longer recital, they were in Ved's room. Leela sat on the single bed. Ved slumped on the desk chair. The light from the lamp was soft. 'So what do you think happened?' he asked anxiously. 'From a woman's point of view?'

'I've got no idea, Ved,' said Leela. 'We're not all telepathically linked at the ovaries.'

'Fuck.' Ved hit his forehead on the desk a few times.

A hand tentatively patted his head. He reached out and pulled Leela on to his lap.

'Shit,' said Ved the next morning. 'I'd forgotten how uncomfortable it is sleeping in a single bed. I like your body though,' he added, feeling Leela's small but shapely bum.

She squirmed onto her back and gazed at the ceiling. 'Ved,' she said. 'Not to state the obvious, but you do realise I never want to do this again?'

Ved sighed. 'That bad?' he said.

'No, I mean, I think you went off in the middle to be sick, but you did brush your teeth afterwards and swallow half a bottle of mouthwash.'

'Oh God,' said Ved. 'Sorry.'

'It's fine. I mean, whatever. But listen, I think I was a bit hard on you yesterday.'

'You think??'

Leela laughed. 'I didn't really like you till just before finals. I thought you were shallow and decent-looking.'

'You thought I was good-looking,' exulted Ved.

She laughed, and got out of bed, locating her underwear. 'Maybe that's why I slept with you. Actually, I think it was more to do with laying to rest the person I used to be when I knew you.'

Ved raised an eyebrow.

'Over-serious,' explained Leela.

'You were very serious,' Ved said. 'That's a bit complicated though. You seem to have slept with some past version of yourself last night.'

Leela finished dressing and chuckled. 'Maybe. Good thing we're all so much better in bed now, I guess. I think I'll go and take a shower. Bye, Ved.'

'Wait! See you at breakfast?' Ved said. 'I'm going to hang around for a bit. Maybe we can get a coffee?'

She stood looking at him.

'I'm not hitting on you,' Ved said. 'It'd actually be nice to hang out for a bit. If you wanted.'

'Okay, sure,' Leela said. 'I wanted to go to the Fitzwilliam, but I guess you could come.'

'I'd like that,' Ved said.

As they walked down Trinity Street a little later, Ved said, 'Did I ask last night what you're up to these days?'

'No,' said Leela.

'What are you up to these days?'

'I do some freelance writing and journalism. Published a novel four years ago. I'm working on another.'

'That's great,' Ved said. 'You used to say you wanted to be a writer. How did the novel do?'

'It did okay,' Leela said. 'It got some nice Amazon reviews, a few blogs. The *Independent* liked it. I was shortlisted for a first novel prize.'

'That's great,' Ved said. 'I guess it's like, art for art's sake? I mean, you're not that focused on success?'

They passed the low overhang of a turret, probably in Caius. Leela laughed. 'You don't worry too much about people's feelings, do you Ved?'

'What?' Ved said. 'I wasn't trying to—look, sorry. You've got to stop being so prickly.'

Leela shuddered. 'I haven't heard that word in years. What does it even mean?'

'It means—look. Calm down, calm down, calm down,' Ved said, waving his hands. They were at the corner of the marketplace. 'Stop assuming that I'm trying to be a dick.'

'What if you're not trying, but I don't like that you *are* a dick?'

Ved inhaled and gazed across the street at King's Chapel, a bleak sky. 'Then forgive me,' he said urgently.

Leela stared.

'Forgive me,' said Ved, not knowing what was coming out of his mouth. 'Forgive me for being crap. Forgive the human race for being disappointing. Forgive me, forgive everyone else, so you don't end up bitter and isolated.' He closed his eyes. 'I may not actually be talking to you,' he admitted, and opened them. A Chinese tourist was taking his picture.

'Probably not,' said Leela. She put her arm through his. 'Come on. Stop being such an exhibitionist.'

They stopped for coffee on the way, and sat on a stone doorstep in Trumpington Street to drink it. Ved sipped his cortado. The cold of the stone crept into his pelvis. He remembered a supervisor who used to joke that Ved, sitting on the stone step outside his rooms before a supervision, would get piles. Or maybe it hadn't been a joke. The whole world right now was solid in a way he wasn't enjoying. Leela sat next to him, drinking her flat white.

'Sorry I'm not making much conversation,' Ved said.

'It's fine,' she said. 'I have my thoughts.'

He glared, and she started laughing. 'This woman really got to you, didn't she? About time.'

'Thanks.'

'Don't mistake me. I don't think a woman needs to save you or anything. Just ...'

'What?' said Ved.

'Life. It happens to everyone. Maybe now it's happening to you.'

'Well, I wish it wouldn't. Let's go, sitting on cold stone gives you piles, Dr Lee used to tell me.'

In the museum, they began on the first floor with the early modern Italian paintings. Ved wandered off. He was looking for something he only half remembered, a brightly coloured tableau ... meanwhile, he gazed at various solemn Madonnas, holding alarmingly middle-aged-looking, dissolute Children. Then he saw it. A strange painting, long like a comic strip, the same figures in different scenes, left to right. It had always intrigued him as well as causing a faint pinch of discomfort. The Story of Cupid and Psyche: Part I, up to the flight of Psyche. There they were, the hidden lovers, first in a cage-like house of their own, with a kid playing on the floor. Then

Cupid flew off and Psyche, blonde and alarmed, floated about in her nightdress. Like Keteki, she glowed—there was a halo of sparkles around her. The sequence was confusing. Psyche appeared to be everywhere, looking distressed.

'What is it you like about this one?' Leela asked. He turned to see her at his side.

'I'm not sure,' Ved said. 'Do you know the story of Cupid and Psyche?'

'No. Do you?'

'Not really,' Ved said. 'It sounds like doomed love though, doesn't it?'

'This is only Part One,' said Leela.

'Yeah,' said Ved. But he felt he could do without the end of the story.

They walked on. 'I like the Breughels,' Leela said.

They peered at a huge canvas in which various people were having a jolly time beating each other up. A couple of skeletons threw one another into a cauldron. 'Nice,' Ved said. 'It's like last night.'

'Simultaneity,' Leela said. 'Everything's happening at once. That's how I feel about time. No past, no future. Just this,' she waved at the Breughel, 'all the time.'

'Hm,' said Ved. He saw himself and Keteki, figures in a story, spread out on a printed tablecloth. How would it end? But perhaps it had never begun, and would never amount to anything.

'Maybe stop being maudlin for, like, a minute,' Leela said.

'Right. Sorry,' said Ved. 'I think, in all honesty, what with the hangover, I've got about fifteen minutes before I need a piece of cake and some coffee. Or lunch and the train.'

'Yeah, let's go,' Leela said.

On the train, she said, 'Ved, I have a feeling—'

'What?' Ved said. He was pretending to read the newspaper.

'With this woman, I think you might have been going about it the wrong way.'

'Yeah?' said Ved. He let his eye rove on a page illustrating overpriced coffee pots. Blue tin, Heal's, one million pounds. Who needed a tin coffee pot? Maybe he should get one.

'You were trying to do the grand gesture, chase her down,' Leela said. She pushed her glasses up her nose. 'But maybe it's better to just—be good at being around. I hesitate to use the word reliable, but I think it's what I mean.'

Ved stared out as the train passed Hitchin. The platform was sodden. 'I think it's a bit late for that,' he said. 'If she'd wanted me to stick around, I don't think Keteki would have scarpered from her uncle's house. And it sounds like I'm not even the first person she's done it to. I think it's fucked.'

'I wonder,' Leela said.

Ved sighed. 'This is a funny time to start being nice.'

She laughed.

At King's Cross, he said, 'It's been so lovely to see you again. Let's—I'll call you.'

'Fuck off, Ved,' said Leela, without rancour. She put up her arms to be hugged.

'Right,' said Ved into her hair. 'Thanks.'

He found himself holding on for longer than he'd intended.

Leela disengaged. She sighed, as though tired of having to say it, but managed, 'It's going to be all right, Ved. Really.'

15

Sand

'KETEKI,' SAID VED. 'Great to see you.' He leaned in to graze her cheek with his.

She had been waiting in the pub for twenty minutes. When he arrived, he was on the phone. He gave her a wave and a smile, but finished the conversation, which didn't sound like work.

'How've you been?' he asked her now. 'What brings you to London? It was a lovely surprise when you called. Hang on, let me get a drink. What would you like? Oh, you already have one.'

Keteki watched him walk to the bar. He was doing her thing—being bluff and light, making it impossible for the other person to set the tone. She sat back and considered. It had been a week since she arrived in England. Four days for the conference, then she'd been at Mark's for two days. She'd called Ved as soon as she was in London, and he had sounded calm and pleased to hear from her. It was more unsettling than if he'd been angry. Why didn't they meet for a drink the following week, he'd suggested. Would she mind coming to Greenwich?

Ved's setting the date of their meeting several days later had meant she'd had time to think about it. This morning, she'd hesitated over what to wear, put on a T-shirt and jeans, then changed into a dress, then back into jeans.

Was Ved better looking in London? If anything, she had imagined he would be less distinct. There were several men of his age in the pub, some with beards, girlfriends and toddlers. But Ved looked good. Was it his skin? His clothes? She had the urge to find a mirror and check her own appearance. But it wasn't a concrete change. After all, when she met Ved in the airport, she hadn't been dressed up. But, importantly, she hadn't been trying.

The windows of the pub gave onto the river, the fronts of grand buildings and a dock. Ved came back with his beer.

'So how are you? Were you out last night?' He nodded at her orange juice.

'Just not drinking that much at the moment,' she said.

'How long are you in town?' His voice and face were only friendly, but he leaned forward. She wondered if his eyes were still eager. 'Did you say,' he went on, 'that you're working with a friend on the pop-up exhibition for the Everlasting Lucifer? Is that a coincidence?'

'Amazing, isn't it? I've worked with Mark before. He got the project; he told me the details after I got here. It'll only be on for ten days, at the Design Museum. Just before the bulb launches, I think. Oh, but you know all that.'

He nodded. 'It's not a full launch, it's more of a trial,' he said. 'Obviously the price will be higher in the UK than in India. But it's still incredibly economical over its lifespan.' He looked down at his hands, then smiled at her. 'So, June again, and we meet in London again.'

Two hours later, she was in Ved's bedroom. He was kissing her and pulling back her hair. She undressed, and sat on the bed. He pulled off his clothes and kneeled. 'Get on your knees,' he said quietly.

When he finished, it was on top of her. She hadn't come. There are so many types of fuck, but she hadn't had this one with him before. What could it be called? The 'I'm in charge' fuck? She looked out through the blinds. A cold grey light off the river, in the Docklands; the cry of a seagull. Everything in the room was the colour of sand: linen sheets, the wooden blinds, a woven matting instead of carpet. There wasn't much clutter: a white shirt on the floor, a lamp, fitted wardrobes and a low bookshelf.

Early in the morning, she woke to find Ved packing a suitcase. 'I have to go to Novgorod this afternoon,' he said.

'Oh!' Keteki said. 'Of course.' She collected her things.

Ved had made coffee. She drank half a cup.

At the door, he said, 'I'll get in touch when I'm back.' Again, the friendly face. 'Speak soon,' he said, closing the door as she left.

'Oh!' said Mark quietly. 'That is not what I thought would happen. I'm sorry, Keteki. Coffee?' He held up the pot.

Keteki followed him into the kitchen. 'Oh well,' she said, as he put the pot on the hob, and lit the gas. 'Disappointment is easier to bear than happiness, don't you think?'

He was pouring milk into a saucepan and laughed so hard that he spilled a little. He reached for a cloth. 'What do you mean? That disappointment is finite?'

'Well,' Keteki said. 'Anything else would just be deferred disappointment, wouldn't it?'

He took off his glasses and wiped his eyes. 'That's so pessimistic,' he said. 'It's as though you can only envisage complete perfection or total disappointment.'

Keteki hesitated. 'You don't think it's true?'

'I don't. There are stages in everything. What about time?'

'Time?' she said doubtfully.

'People change,' Mark said. 'Things develop. Maybe Ved is trying to play it cool, or giving you a taste of your own medicine.'

When he handed her the coffee, she smiled and thanked him. They went to the living room, where sketches and plans were laid out on the large tables, with images showing some of the stages in the exhibition, and a moodboard.

'I have a couple of meetings this afternoon,' Mark said. 'Do you want to come?'

Keteki considered. 'I think I'd like to do something simple and repetitive,' she said.

He laughed. 'Well, I'd be so grateful if you could file some of the receipts and papers we've been stuffing in that box file in a more methodical way.'

Keteki spent a quiet afternoon. It was so peaceful to organise something abstract, so terrifying to try to put one's own life in order. When she finished, she leafed through the picture books on one of the tables. There was a catalogue from the Hokusai exhibition. A whole page showed enormous carp, leaping in a waterfall. The water was depicted in straight lines, opaque colour, as though it had been a solid object. She sat looking at it for a while. What was being represented, she realised, was the light on the water, not the water itself.

The carp were monstrous, their florid tails and grotesque heads protruding. It wasn't realism, but reality too was more grotesque than people liked to believe.

She wandered down the main road, looking in shop windows without desire. When she dropped into a yoga studio to ask about classes, they offered a month's trial. The next morning, her mind clear, she worked through sun salutations, standing poses, forward bends, twists. A man next to her sweated in just a pair of shorts. The teacher appeared, and leaned the whole of her body onto Keteki's back until she was folded into paschimottanasana, West on Top pose, her face sweetly mashed into her knees. Expectant, silent, she breathed.

16

Not so Wil. E.

VED WAS MAKING dinner. 'Let's see what we have,' he said, and opened the fridge. 'There's some salmon. Cherry tomatoes. Pesto.' He looked in a cupboard. 'New potatoes.'

'It sounds like a meal,' Keteki said. She was sitting on the wide windowsill in his open living room kitchen, looking out.

Ved frowned. 'I don't normally ... this feels a bit more domesticated than I usually ...' He took out the salmon and opened the packet, looked with some disdain at the plastic film, and spent a while trying to fold it up and put it in the bin. 'Hey, you know the key I gave you,' he began, suddenly, while irritated about the fact that he had to rinse two pieces of oily fish.

'Yes,' said Keteki, not turning, still looking out of the window.

'I need it back,' said Ved, putting on his deepest voice and clipped tones. 'Karolina, ah, who comes to do the housekeeping, I think she's misplaced her key.'

'Sure,' Keteki said, unfolding her legs and getting down from the windowsill. She looked around for her bag and came back with the key, put it on the counter in front of Ved.

'Thanks,' Ved said. 'Drink?'

'Sure.'

She sat at a bar stool on the other side of the kitchen island, and he took out a bottle and poured two glasses. 'It's nice wine,' Keteki said. The kitchen island was brightly lit; she kept looking over towards the windows.

'What are you looking at?' said Ved.

'Oh, well, I guess, just the long evenings,' she said. 'It's not new, but it always feels so different.'

Ved looked at her, remembered the bar in the lounge at Heathrow, and then said, 'I met my ex-girlfriend, when I was on my way to Russia. I hadn't seen her in years. We were together when I was in college. She—her name is Safia.' He was aware of sounding stagey. 'We broke up just before we graduated. I hadn't seen her since then. She looked great. She's doing very well.'

'That's nice,' said Keteki, looking into her wine glass.

'I don't think she likes me very much,' Ved said, with some discomfort. He tried not to think about the encounter, in which, just before she left, Safia had asked Ved what had happened, why he'd ended things and seemed so cold right before they were to graduate. Ved had thought of the truth, which was that he thought he had a chance with a tall, disdainful girl with red hair who read English at another college, and also that he'd been young and stupid. 'I'm sorry,' he said to Safia. 'It wasn't personal.' Not an answer that had impressed her.

Keteki looked at him. Ved finished putting the salmon, wrapped in foil, into the oven, and shrugged. 'I think I fucked up there,' he said.

'You wish you'd stayed together?'

Ved shrugged. 'I just think I fucked up,' he said. He remembered something else. 'Oh, there are some rumbles of problems now, with the Lucifer. I've been getting emails about incidents where the bulbs are bursting. It doesn't make any sense, unless the testing was less thorough than it seemed, or maybe there was some problem in the distribution chain.'

'That's unfortunate.'

'It is. I'm going to talk to Ganesh about it tomorrow, early in the morning. We might have to delay the launch, or something.' He exhaled. 'Nothing's ever simple, is it?'

Keteki had got up and was washing the potatoes under the tap. 'No,' she said. 'Nothing's ever simple.'

'Keteki,' said Mark the next afternoon, 'let's finish up now. I'm going for a walk, do you want to come? Or are you going to Ved's?'

'Not today,' Keteki said. 'There are some problems with the Lucifer, he's talking to the CEO about it. Maybe Ved will have to go to India, so they can figure out what to do about the launch.'

Mark nodded. 'Walk?' he suggested.

They left the apartment building, crossed the main road, turned down a side lane, and were soon in streets of tall, Dutch-looking houses, unforgiving with their regularly spaced windows like eyes. Keteki thought of Uzan Bazar, the tiny countrified lanes leading to the river, a woman outside her house in winter, burning paper at the side of the road and the scent of smoke in the chilly air.

'How's everything?' Mark said. 'You seem a little glum. How's it going with Ved?'

'I don't know,' Keteki said. She heard the unhappiness in her own voice and felt startled. 'He's ... I ... maybe I seem less interesting to him now that I'm actually here. We have a good time, a lot of the time, just talking, or making dinner, or something really simple.'

'That sounds positive,' Mark said.

'Yes,' Keteki said. 'I can't make it out. I feel like I'm suspended, waiting for him to do something, but maybe it's just that I normally avoid getting anywhere near as close as this to any kind of—' She waved her hand. They crossed another road and turned.

Mark smiled. 'Relationship may be the word you're looking for.'

'When I was in the yoga ashram ... I was telling you about it the other night,' Keteki began.

'It sounds like a wonderful experience.'

'It was strange, but when I was there, I had so much time to sift through things. Difficult things from the past and even to think about what I really want to do ... with my life.' She laughed. 'That sounds very earnest, but I think I want to start taking some things seriously. Even a relationship, starting something of my own, the textile project I was talking about, working with a few weavers. I've never wanted to get involved in structure, or take responsibility for something before.'

They passed large, forbidding mansion blocks like prisons.

'The idea of a relationship basically fills me with dread,' said Keteki. 'Like in the cartoons, you know, when they're chasing someone, and they go over a cliff and there's this moment of just hanging there, looking down. Roadrunner. Who's the one who chases Roadrunner?'

Mark laughed. 'Yosemite Sam.'

'Oh no, I didn't mean him. Isn't there another one? I can't be a little redneck fur trapper, that's a bit much.'

'Wile E. Coyote?'

Keteki laughed. 'Yes. That's such a great name. In Assam, there are stories about a character called Teton Tamuli. He's continually trying to con other people, but often ends up doing things that turn out worse for him. I guess I don't want to be Teton Tamuli any more, I don't want to keep trying to win just by trying to be cunning. But I also— Once you get involved with someone or something and take it seriously, isn't it just splat?'

Mark laughed again. 'You're such a reluctant lover.'

They were on the embankment now, passing a couple on a bench.

'And what about Ved, do you think he's ready for a relationship?'

'I've no idea,' Keteki said. 'I thought— That's what he said, the last time we were together, but then I ran away. Now I'm mainly so terrified at the idea of it myself that I just sit around, not saying much, waiting for the nightmare to happen.'

They walked up to the bridge, which was brightly lit in the early evening.

'What's the nightmare?'

'Oh, getting hurt, being left, or being … someone doing me harm, I guess. Being left behind.'

'Shall we walk across the bridge?' Mark said. She took his arm. 'What is it about Ved?' he asked. 'I mean, you've always seemed so … self-possessed till now.'

'Is that loathsome?' Keteki wondered.

He smiled, as though at an indignant child. 'Enviable,' he said.

There was a fresh wind in their faces now. Keteki looked east, to the left, and then right, where the sunset was most colourful. 'I learned,' she said. 'When I was much younger. To be self-contained. At boarding school, then at Oxford. Before that, you could see everything in my face. I wasn't—No one really saw me as a child. Not really.'

Mark nodded.

'My mother was really beautiful,' she went on. 'A little mad, too intense. She never saw things from anyone else's point of view. She was always convinced you were doing something wrong, that everyone was betraying her. But she was so beautiful, no one could resist her. I really don't know … The first time I met Ved, it was obvious he was interested in me, and I, it wasn't anything like love at first sight, or even intense attraction. I just thought he was quite nice-looking, and I liked him. I thought he was harmless, if that makes any sense. Now I feel like I'm in love with him, and I'm frightened of whatever he's thinking or whether he's lost interest. I really don't know anything about him, I don't know who he is. Maybe he's met someone else.'

They had reached the other bank. They turned around to walk over the bridge again.

'The first time I fell in love,' Mark said, 'it was with a boy. But if I talk about it now, to most people, I say it was a woman, I say my first girlfriend.'

'Why?' Keteki said.

'We were best friends too. We were in school together. Then, when I went to university, we were a couple, but we never really came out or anything. I think he didn't want to. We were so young, we lived together as though we were just best friends. And then, after it ended, I fell in love with a woman, and we were together for ten years. Two children.' He looked at Keteki.

'You have children?'

Mark smiled. 'I'll show you photographs when we get back. Amy—their mother—wanted to emigrate to New Zealand. So, I don't see them often. But we Skype.'

'I didn't even realise,' Keteki murmured. 'I guess we've worked together before, but we've never spent so much time together.'

He squeezed her arm briefly. 'It's been good to have the company. I always like working with you. Maybe you're lucky for me. Don't worry too much about Ved. Maybe he's so used to chasing, he doesn't know what to do beyond that.'

'I don't know,' Keteki said. She felt her phone vibrate, and took it out of her pocket. 'It's Ved,' she said, reading a text. 'He's at the airport, on his way to Assam.'

After he left, Ved didn't text or call. For over a week, Keteki lived more at night than in the day. The nights were alive with fear and disaster. She drank in the evening, relaxed a little, then awoke after an hour, dry-mouthed. Something bad was happening. She saw Ved moaning, getting a blow job, or fucking a shapely woman from behind. In all the nightmares, he was more intent, more present than he'd ever been with her.

In the morning, she got up late after a few hours of sleep, made coffee, read the notes Mark had left her with, numbered lists of reminders: light boxes, caption texts, press release.

Three days after Ved had flown to India, Keteki reflected on the irony. It had been a long time since she was the person left behind. She thought of an afternoon in Oxford ... or was it a series of afternoons now compressed into one? The day was grey, and there was a soapy cup of instant coffee next to her, a pile of books on the table. She lay on her bed, thinking about the boy she was sleeping with. He had stopped calling, and wandered off with someone else, though he never got around to telling Keteki. A few days later, red-faced, she ran into them in town, holding hands.

Twenty years later, that early experience of rejection seemed so cosy. Strange that you spent so long protecting yourself from uncomfortable feelings, until they surged up with new intensity.

Sometimes she could see Ved was online, but she didn't hear from him though she'd messaged once or twice. She went through indifference, rage, sadness, despair, incredulity, rage again, an attempt to reason herself back to indifference, gibbering terror, and finally, past the point of struggle, she realised she couldn't do it any longer. She phoned Mark, who was at the site, and went to meet him for lunch.

'I'm feeling better,' she said. 'I'm sorry about the last week.'

He patted her on the shoulder, and carried on chewing his halloumi wrap. 'I didn't know you were so volatile,' he said. 'It's nice.'

Keteki laughed and sighed. 'I'm wrung out,' she said. 'It's the new normal.'

'What is?'

'Sleeplessness,' she said. 'Feeling terrible. I'm like a teenager. Although I wasn't actually like this as a teenager.'

He smiled. 'It's quite sexy, you know.'

'I don't think so,' she said. 'I look hideous.' She put down her sandwich; she'd eaten half of it. Any more, and she'd fall asleep where she sat.

In the afternoon, under fluorescent light, she checked the alignment of the captions. Everything was askew. It was beautiful, though, to fix her mind to details. After the electrician left, they did a walk through.

The visitor would first enter the exhibition space under a skylight. A shaft of daylight fell on him as he began his journey.

'Will they even notice it?' Mark asked. He'd liked Keteki's plan for the story that unfolded in the labyrinth-like path.

'But does it make sense to label it?' she'd wondered. In the end, they put up a sign: 'Natural light, London, today.'

In the next alcove, there was a rocking chair and a standard lamp with a Lucifer in it. It was hard not to feel that the Lucifer glowed more finely, more golden, than the daylight. Then the space opened into a series of objects and pictures: the old Lucifer advertisements; 'What is a filament?' with a giant filament on display; and, near the end, a photograph of the Phiringoti Devi shrine at the Moran factory. 'I'm not sure about that,' Mark said. He pointed out that the Assam factory was one of two, and the Goddess of Sparks might not mean as much to an English museum-goer. But Ganesh Appaiah of Lucifer & Co. liked the idea. He and his family were supposed to come to London to see the little exhibition, though that was now less certain. There was still no word from Ved.

She went back to Mark's, and on exiting the underground, got a message from Tom, a friend whose parents lived in Suffolk. He and a few friends were planning to spend the weekend there and go to a pub on an island in a river. There'd be an evening of traditional folk music. 'It'll be relaxed, super fun,' he said. 'Hope you can make it.'

The morning she was due to leave, Keteki woke early, as though a bird had rapped at her window. But there was no message, just the daylight, more prosaic than for the last nine days. Buildings looked like buildings; the street was just a street, grey and cool. She made coffee, took a shower, and twenty minutes later, was standing outside the apartment block. From down the street she got a waft of washing detergent and steam; there were London sounds, a delivery truck reversing, the click of a woman's heels.

A very old, low-slung blue car drew up.

'Hey there,' Keteki said. She grinned. Tom was the same, licks of grey at his sideburns. His eyes were lazy and deep. 'Kato,' he said.

Keteki chucked her holdall in the back, got into the front, folded her legs, put on her seat belt. They pulled away.

'So good to see you,' she said.

Music was playing, gentle rap with an acoustic guitar.

'This is nice, what is it?' Keteki asked.

Tom turned the car towards the museums. 'It's Immortal Technique,' he said. 'I think the song's called "Leaving the Past."' He grinned at her. 'We're going via the North Circular, I'm afraid. It's not too scenic, but it's the quickest route right now.'

'Scenic in a different way,' Keteki said a little while later. They were driving past furniture depots. She blinked. Something large and white rose over the brown cube of a warehouse. It was a hot air balloon, tethered to the building. The balloon was printed to look like a white light bulb, and on it, dancing around the silver filament, with the legend Everlasting Lucifer, was a cartoon devil. Keteki's phone buzzed in her pocket. She took it out. Ved had sent her a picture. For a moment the icon whirled, indicating process. Then there was a photo of a handsome, grey-haired man lifting a glass of beer to the camera and smiling. Her uncle.

17

The Rushcutters

'So how have you been? How are things?' Keteki smiled at her friend. She had a can of apple juice and a bag of crisps; there was music, the weather was good and she'd stopped feeling dread. All she wanted was to stay like this.

'Things are … good,' Tom said. He smiled, then stared ahead.

'Work?'

'Yeah, really picking up. You know what it's like when you're freelance, but I've had some great jobs come in. Redoing a pub in West London, they're making it into a gastropub.'

'Oh, that's great.'

'Yeah. Laura and I split up.' His eyes, hazel and alive, met hers.

'Oh shit. I'm sorry.'

'Oh,' he shrugged, lifted his hands from the wheel and let them drop again. 'Fuck it, Kato.'

Keteki laughed. 'I forgot you called me that.'

'You don't remember that time at Woody's?'

Keteki was thrown. 'In our second year? Come on.' Jeff Woodward, a year above them in college, lived in North

Oxford. At Easter, when his parents were away, he had a house party that went on for a long weekend. Late one night, Tom and Keteki chased each other around the house pretending to be Clouseau and Cato from the *Pink Panther*. At some point, they realised no one else was in the game and, in Woody's neurologist dad's study, had sex behind the leather sofa. Twice.

'I've often wondered why didn't we just fuck *on* the sofa,' Tom said now.

Keteki smiled and looked at a sign marking the turning for Saffron Walden. 'Did they ever actually grow saffron in Saffron Walden?' she murmured.

Tom laughed. His crow's feet came out and his brown face flushed. 'You're changing the subject,' he noted.

'I'm sorry about you and Laura,' Keteki said.

'Ah well. It was great. She's a great person.'

'She is.' Keteki had liked Laura, though they never became friends. Perhaps because of that time at Woody's. Or maybe, she diverted herself with this, because they were both tall. How absurd. But if nothing was real, why should it not also be ridiculous? She smiled at the old car's dashboard. The dashboard hummed back at her, as if enjoying the joke.

'What are you musing on, Kato?'

'Good music, nice car, lovely to see you,' Keteki said. 'Everything is alive. I do need to pee though.'

'I'll stop at the next services,' Tom promised. 'You can have a wee, we'll get a coffee, I'll have a cigarette.'

An hour and a half later, they drew into the drive of Tom's parents' house. Another car was parked near the door.

'Oh, Pete and Elsa said they might arrive a bit earlier,' Tom said.

'How did they get in?' Keteki asked.

'There's a key under the fourth plant pot to the left in the greenhouse. Now you're back in the country, it might be good to keep that in mind.'

'Where are your parents again?'

'Thailand, Vietnam, Laos, Cambodia. I don't think they'll be back for Christmas.'

Keteki helped him unpack the car, and they went into the large house. In the porch was a congregation of wellingtons and shoes, and then from the hall onwards, a variety of rugs and pictures on every wall. The dog appeared, a Collie-Labrador cross, Dexter, barking with joy. He thrust his thin face at Keteki, putting his arms on hers, and she hugged him.

'Hey!' Pete and Elsa came out of the kitchen. Pete was holding a bottle.

'You're drinking,' Keteki said.

'Just a beer. The sun's over the yard arm.'

Elsa laughed. 'At one o'clock?' she said.

Keteki followed them into the kitchen, a large room with a pine table, a huge dresser, and on the wall next to the table, a green tapestry that she remembered from her last visit. 'I love that,' she said.

'It's beautiful, isn't it,' Elsa said. 'I think Tom's mother bought it.'

'It's contemporary, but they're cutting rushes,' Keteki said. The figure in the foreground of the tapestry was bending and scything green stems; behind him, another man was tying bundles of reeds. In the background, a third person, a woman, was loading the bundles into a low boat, heaped with reeds that hung over the sides, resembling hair. Near the first figure, a dragonfly hazed past; there were butterflies too, and a sickle resting on the bank. The figures weren't archaic: the woman near the boat wore dungarees and had short hair. But there was a faded quality to the tapestry that seemed to have appeared over a long time. A languor in the figures made it seem as though the scene had taken place long ago, or more mysteriously, been observed much earlier even though it had happened only recently.

Keteki yawned.

'Sit down,' Pete said. 'Have a beer.'

'I'd pass out,' she said.

'Do you want to take a nap?' Elsa asked. 'We're putting lunch together.'

Keteki squeezed Elsa's arm and went to look for a place to curl up. She peeked into the dining room, then found the den, with a battered velvet sofa, bookshelves and doors into the garden. It reminded her of the book room in Jorhat. She stretched out on the sofa under a blanket, a copy of the *Observer* magazine next to her. Her body began to shimmer and evaporate; she was watching a man in waterproof trousers standing in a clear river, scything and lifting bunches of heavy reeds. She was aware, too, of an iridescent blue dragonfly, moving around the man. Every element of the scene was alive, electively present: water, earth, rushes, air, the dragonfly.

A moment later, she felt the lightest of stroking on her scalp, until her head floated away from her body, drifting upwards. Her awareness was yearningly on the stroking, fearing it might end, before it turned into a simple hum of bliss.

Eventually the fingers lifted, and she was aware of a heavy leg leaning on hers.

'Lunch,' Tom said. He was on the sofa, knees bent, and he rested his hand on her shoulder. Keteki sat up a little awkwardly, detached herself and smiled. He put an arm around her as they walked into the kitchen.

'Oh, wow,' Keteki said. The table was laid and Elsa was putting a circular baking tray down. 'What's that? It smells amazing.'

Elsa smiled. 'I just used what we could find. Onion and jalapeno quiche with parmesan.' She took off her apron and sat down.

'Delicious,' said Tom a few mouthfuls later.

'So good,' Keteki said.

Pete smiled. 'I live with her.'

'That's all kinds of happiness,' Keteki said, nodding to him. 'Are you guys in Cambridge now?'

They lived outside the city, in a village near the veterinary practice where Elsa worked.

'You just came back, right?' she said.

'Not long ago. I'm just here for a month or two,' Keteki said.

'Hm,' Elsa said. 'England. I guess sometimes I miss knowing how to deal with people. In Finland, people are direct. Pete's family are so nice to me. But I don't always understand what they are saying: "Oh, that would be lovely", "No, don't worry about it", all that.' She laughed. 'Finnish people are strange, I know. We are probably not that friendly, especially to outsiders. It's just—'

'You're used to the shape of strangeness in your own place,' Keteki suggested.

'Yes, something like that. But I love my work. I get to work with horses as well as small animals. And it's been great, with Pete.' She waved towards her boyfriend. 'You know, when we met, he wasn't really looking for a relationship. And

I wasn't sure if I would stay in England. For a while, when we were first together— How long was it?' She turned to Pete.

'Not that long,' he said. 'Just at the beginning.'

'A few *months*,' said Elsa. 'I didn't know what was happening. I thought maybe it would just turn out to be a short thing.'

'Well, it was early,' Pete said mildly.

'I know,' Elsa said. 'But it was frustrating. And then,' she turned to Keteki and Tom, 'when it seemed like Pete was getting attached to me, I felt so confused. Maybe I liked the idea of winning him over. I didn't know what to do when there was no resistance. I was like a car with the engine revving but the back wheels off the ground.'

'I love this place,' Keteki said. It was early evening in the Rushcutters. The walls of the snug back room were panelled in a way she'd never seen before, four kinds of wood inlaid in interwoven spirals.

'Snakes,' said Elsa, tracing one with a finger.

'What's everyone drinking?' Pete came back from the bar, where Tom was waiting.

'Cold lager, please,' Elsa said cheerfully.

'Same for me, please,' Keteki said.

She and Elsa were sitting in the snug when Tom's voice seemed to come out of the corner behind them. They heard his laugh, a growly cackle Keteki had always liked.

He said, 'Stay over another night.'

Then Pete's softer voice, 'No mate, we have to go back tomorrow. Work.'

'The sound in this room is really strange,' Elsa said.

Keteki had a sense of the pub, which was a simple, old-fashioned house, as a vortex, warm, soaking in its own time period. Even the walls seemed to vibrate with it. 'I'm going to take a look around,' she told Elsa, and went outside.

At the water's edge, she sat down and leaned back on her hands. The intense feeling was diffused here; she heard some tourists laughing and talking about the boat they'd arrived in. The sun was warm on her face, and she got up to stop herself falling asleep, and kept walking.

The pub had been built in the sixteenth century as a mill-keeper's cottage, and the mill pond was at the back. A man stood there, smoking and staring into the water. Keteki turned to leave, then turned back. The thin, dark-haired stranger smiled, secretive, as though expressing her mood. He opened his mouth, but checked himself.

Keteki looked round.

'There you are,' Tom said. He raised an eyebrow. 'Running away already?'

Keteki smiled. He held a beer and a glass of Pimm's. 'Yes, my policy is always to get the girliest drink possible,' he said. He handed her the beer and eyed the dark-haired stranger. 'Come inside?' he said to Keteki. 'The music's going to start soon.'

'In that case,' said the other man, who appeared to be Irish, 'I'd better come in too, since I'm the music.' He smiled at Keteki. 'Neil O'Halloran.'

She shook the outstretched hand. 'Keteki Sharma,' she said.

'Tom Hurst,' said Tom, putting out his hand. Keteki looked at the two of them, Tom stocky and scruff in jeans and faded T-shirt, and the musician, pale as a ghost, his hair dark. He wore an old black T-shirt, a checked shirt, black drainpipe jeans, boots.

'Well,' he said. 'I should probably go in.'

Tom and Keteki looked at each other. The rushing of the water into the pond was loud, and the light was changing.

'Right,' Tom said, 'let's go and hear our new friend play his songs?'

She followed him in.

'... please give a warm welcome to Neil O'Halloran!' The huge landlord was just stepping away from the microphone.

The thin Irishman smiled. He was sitting on a stool in the corner. 'Thank you very much, Thaddeus,' he said. 'Thank you for having me and me guitar. This is a beautiful place, and it's a beautiful summer's eve ... and I just met a beautiful Indian girl out by the mill pond.' He looked at Keteki. She was sitting on a stool next to the table. The unusual acoustics of the square room brought his voice past her, so that it appeared to be whispering in her ear from behind, as though they were already in bed.

'St Patrick is said to have banished all the snakes from Ireland,' Neil said. 'Though I've also heard we've no fossils showing there ever *were* any snakes, so maybe it was the easiest miracle ever,' and the now full room laughed. Keteki looked around: there were men with generous bellies, perched on high stools, and women with faces that had weathered storms, sunshine and years of disappointingly grey days.

'But this is a song about snakes, about beginnings that are endings, about biting your own tail, something I know I've ... ah, I'll just sing, I think.' The last few words died into a murmur, and to more chuckles, he began to play. His voice was delicate and wavering. 'The first time I saw you, the last time we met …'

Keteki sat in a hum of pleasantness, following the voice, both impressed and horrified by the extrovert's need to be vulnerable in front of an audience. But perhaps he felt not vulnerable but at home, like slipping into a river on a hot day. When she and her cousins had been children, there was a tiny beach near the snake temple where local kids would swim. Some days, the water was blue like a picture of a tropical sea. Until you got in, water, land and sky all seemed distinct. But as you entered the river, feeling the cold, delightful slippage against your skin, the water was revealed as living and many: there were tiny fish, suspended particles. Sunlight entered the top layers, insects flew above the river, and clumps of fleshy-leaved meteka drifted by. She remembered feeling her own self, too, as many, each limb diverse, each thought individual, even its life was a brief flash.

Clapping, and the song had ended. Neil was gazing at Keteki. She smiled; he mouthed, 'Beautiful'. Keteki saw Tom twitch, but by the time she turned, he was again in profile. The music went on, and she listened, aware of her friends behind her, all of them floating in the stream of things. The singer, whose name she'd already forgotten … Will? No, Neil, that was it. Her eyes landed on him, focused uncertainly, and he looked back. There was a moment of contact—or was it emptiness?

Another song, louder and more strummy, with an insistent refrain: 'And I'll see you again before you go.' Cheers from the audience. Elsa came back from the bar, with beer for everyone. Keteki tried to catch Tom's eye, but he was too far away. She gave up and sipped her beer, then went in search of the bathroom. While she was waiting for a cubicle, she heard two women discussing Neil. 'He's hot,' said one.

'His legs are skinny,' said the other one. 'I wouldn't kick him out of bed though.'

When they emerged, Keteki was only slightly surprised that they were younger than her, and attractive. She examined herself in the unforgiving light and saw a scruffy T-shirt, pores, lines near her mouth and white hairs madly spidering from the sides of her head. What could the Irishman have been thinking? Maybe he had a thing for foreigners. She smirked, and in a flash saw the mirror image, the sides of her eyes becoming an upward slanting line: she was Joy mama, but also her eldest uncle, Sandeep mama. Quickly, she turned away.

While she was at the bar, someone touched her elbow. 'Hi,' said a soft voice.

Keteki turned. 'Oh, hi,' she said. 'You were great, well done.'

The Irishman nodded. 'Were you bored?'

'Oh no no no.' She waved her hand, and clutched his surprisingly substantial upper arm. 'Not at all.'

He smiled wryly. 'Folk music isn't for everyone. My ex-girlfriend called it Those Dirges.'

Keteki laughed. 'Maybe it's for the best she's an ex.' She leaned her elbow on the bar. It was easy to talk this way, uninvolved. In her pocket, her phone buzzed. She ignored it.

'Tired?' Neil asked.

'*Super* tired,' she said, and pushed back her hair. 'I'm working with a friend, we're doing a pop-up exhibition for a lighting company, they're putting out a new product, so it's looking at their history. It's nice because it's an Indian company and they have a lovely archive. It's like a history of advertising in the early twentieth century.'

'Sounds amazing,' Neil said. 'Is that what you do, stuff for companies?'

Keteki shrugged. 'Mostly it's more like fine art or an exhibition with a theme. I used to do some textile design. I want to get back to that but—'

The bar was noisy; a tall red-faced man came up to shake Neil's hand. 'Lovely music,' he said. 'Which part of Ireland are you from? My mother's from County Clare.'

'I'm from Kerry,' Neil said.

'That's lovely country,' said the other man.

Keteki began to melt away, but a hand grabbed her T-shirt from behind. 'I just want to check on my friends,' she said.

'Can I come meet them?'

'You already met Tom.' She smiled apologetically at the tall man, who looked admiring.

'I don't think he likes me,' complained Neil.

Keteki raised an eyebrow. 'He likes everyone. I really—'

'I'll be over in a second,' he said.

'Then can you bring this pint? It's for Tom.'

She made her way back to their table. Pete was in conversation with a man in overalls, who reminded Keteki of someone.

'Hi,' she said, and gave Pete his beer.

'Ian Swanton,' said the other man. He had a deep voice.

'Ian works as a rushcutter,' Pete said.

'That's so interesting,' Keteki said. She looked across her shoulder to the corner where Tom and Elsa were talking intently. Tom raised a glass to Keteki, and Elsa looked irritated. Keteki found she could hear murmurs of their talk because of the peculiar quality of the wooden panelling.

Tom's voice, lower, but also tight, '… no, that's a terrible idea …'

Elsa, her voice sweet but forceful with frustration, 'I just think the right thing to do is tell him.'

Keteki stopped listening and focused on the man in overalls. 'We make various things,' he was saying, 'but rush matting is the main one. It's been in use since medieval times, you know. Now people like it because it's eco-friendly and local.'

'Like the tapestry,' Keteki said.

Neil appeared, delivered Tom's pint, and sat next to Keteki. 'You were telling me about your work,' he said. He put a hand on her arm.

'It's erratic,' she said. 'Projects here and there.'

'Sounds like my life,' he said. As he talked, Keteki gazed at him. What pretty eyes he had, a dark line underneath like eyeliner. She got lost in mapping the points of stubble on his face, blue where they were still under the skin. What was it about beards? An infantile fascination with the father? She had spent so little time with hers. A memory of a photo, her father handsome in an eri silk shirt and rust-coloured flares, sideburns and a moustache. He was holding a gurgling Keteki, aged just under two.

Neil was saying, '… touring, moving around, it's far from glamorous. It's hard to maintain relationships, even keep up with your friends, you know?'

Keteki made an understanding face. 'Excuse me for a minute,' she said, and made her way without urgency through the large, happy bodies filling the two outer bars, and towards the toilets. While she waited for a cubicle, she looked at her phone. Ved had sent a series of messages. 'How are you?' said one, not a question he often asked, and a sign therefore of desperation. 'Missing you,' said another. She'd waited over a week for a sign of life from him. She washed her hands over-thoroughly.

While she was on her way back to the snug, the front door of the pub opened, and a hugely tall, very broad young man came in, his face stormy. He was dressed head-to-toe in sap green: a jersey and leggings. He pushed past Keteki, and one of the other three young men in green who followed him glanced at her and stopped to say, 'Sorry about that.'

Keteki's gaze followed the other three. The backs of their jerseys said Green Knights Cycling Team.

'It's for charity,' explained the young man who'd stopped. He had sandy hair and an appealing face. 'Geraint, who bumped into you, he lost his brother to a degenerative muscle disease in April, so we did a five-hundred-mile charity ride to raise money.'

'I'm sorry about his brother,' Keteki said. 'There was music earlier,' she went on. 'But you missed it.'

'Oh, there's generally a lock-in at the Rushcutters,' said the sandy-haired young man. 'I'm Albert.'

'Keteki.'

'Nice to meet you, Katy. What brings you here?'

'I'm doing some work in London,' Keteki said. 'I came for the weekend. My friend Tom's parents live nearby, in Great Morton.'

'Tom Hurst? I know Tom,' exclaimed Albert. 'He was in my brother's year at school. Is he here?'

'At the back, in the little wooden room,' Keteki began.

'Oh, that's the whettle room,' said Albert. 'Back in a minute.'

Keteki went into the garden. At the water's edge, near a picnic table, she found a dog gazing at the dark river. 'Hello,' she said, and sat down near the dog, but not too near, so as to respect its space. The river flowed, making slapping and sucking sounds. She thought of last year, in the monsoon, when she and her friend Lueit had gone to north Guwahati, where the beach had vanished into high waters, and of the evening she'd spent with Ved on the riverbank at Uzan Bazar, the sky flaring into sunset, the air smoky. The grass felt damp beneath her, and she could feel the evening cool down and thin out, a fraying of all that was warm and estival as the indoor world solidified and massed.

Voices, a sound of oars.

'No, that's not right. I'm telling you …'

'Fuck that.' This voice sounded younger.

'Look, Andrew, be reasonable.'

Keteki stiffened. Something about that older voice …

A rowing boat came into view, and a thin figure, crouching, leaned out to throw a rope over a mooring peg on the lawn. Then he got out and offered a hand to the other man. Keteki watched him stand, tall, broad-shouldered. The boat lurched. 'Jesus, Andrew,' complained the older man.

'It's not my fault,' insisted the youth. 'You're drunk.'

With a final stumble, the heavier man attained the lawn. 'Fuck's sake,' he said. He leaned on the teenager's shoulder and they walked into the pub. Keteki was pretty sure the older man was Jonathan Carlisle, then a twenty-six-year-old graduate student struggling to finish his DPhil, who'd broken her heart when she was nineteen. He was still only seven years older than Keteki, presumably, but she felt as though they had been ageing at different speeds.

The dog got up and walked into the pub. After a while, beset by the urge to talk to someone, Keteki followed. Neil waved as she came in, but she looked around for Tom. She couldn't see him in the front bar, and the back room was heaving. She went left. The tall red-faced man loomed near the doorway. 'Hello,' said Keteki.

'How are you doing?' he asked.

'I'm having a very strange evening,' she admitted. 'Although maybe it's just that I've hardly slept in the last week.'

He held out his hand. 'Richard Kerrigan.' He pointed at a table in the side bar. 'What's been keeping you awake, if I might ask?'

Keteki sighed and sat down. 'It's so boring. A man. I can't explain how much I dislike myself for saying that.'

Richard Kerrigan had an impish laugh. 'Isn't that a bit extreme?' he said. 'We're all human.'

Keteki stared at the broad backs of drinkers in the middle bar. 'I suppose I thought I was good at not caring,' she said.

He smiled. 'Let me get us a whisky.' A few minutes later, he returned with two tumblers. 'Now,' he said, 'I have a question, but I hope you'll be honest. The lock-in has begun, but would you mind if I smoked?'

Keteki grinned. 'Not if you let me bum one.'

He rolled two cigarettes, and passed her one.

'It's nice to have a hobby that's going nowhere,' she mused.

'Or only in one direction,' he said.

She inhaled, laughed, coughed and nodded.

'You said you hadn't slept in a week, why is that?' he asked.

Keteki smoked, aware of the cigarette marking time, and grateful for it. 'I guess I was worrying that this man doesn't, well …' she said.

'That he doesn't love you?'

She nodded.

He thought. 'How could he not?'

She rolled her eyes. 'You're very kind, but …'

He looked at her and took a sip. 'I'm sorry,' he said. 'It's been a while since I was in the grip of this sort of feeling. I do remember it though.'

'He went away about a week ago,' Keteki said. She tried the whisky. It was smoky and good. 'I thought I was dying, but very slowly. I didn't hear from him, I couldn't sleep. And he did eventually get back in touch. But it was all so degrading. I don't want to feel like that.'

'Oho, so he hasn't disappeared?'

Keteki shrugged.

Richard Kerrigan smiled. 'If something is affecting you this intensely, maybe it's not just about this man. But as far as he's concerned, I think men fall in love differently. At first it's mainly about how the woman looks.' He smoked and thought. 'After a while, there's a time of pulling back a little. Actually getting to know her. And that's when the real falling in love happens.'

'God, how annoying,' said Keteki.

There were cries from elsewhere. 'What *time* is it?' she asked.

'Sounds like trouble in the whettle room,' Richard Kerrigan said. For a big man, he was up quickly. 'I'd better go and see if Thaddeus needs any help.'

Keteki looked at his half-empty glass, hesitated, then drank his whisky and got up to follow him in the direction of the whettle room. In the doorway, she walked straight into Jonathan Carlisle.

'Sorry,' she said, and backed away. Their eyes met.

'Sorry,' he said, but didn't move aside completely.

Keteki smirked and walked past him.

'Wait!' he said. 'Don't I know you?'

Her eyes slid away.

'Ketecky,' he said.

'Hi,' she said.

'You look great. Er, Jonathan? From Oxford? Merton?'

'*Jon*athan. Of course. How are you?' She laughed inwardly.

He passed a hand over his head. 'Bit of a mess, honestly. Let's have a drink. Are you here with someone?'

'I was just going to find my friends,' Keteki said. 'Great to see you.'

'Wait! Are you in the UK?' His eyes narrowed. 'We should— Tell you what. You go and find them and come back. I'll be here.' He rumpled her hair and gave her a distracted beam. 'I'll tell you all about everything when you get back.'

Keteki smiled and hurried through the front bar, her eyebrows raised. It had been twenty years, and he wanted to tell her about his problems.

On her way to the whettle room, she finally saw Tom. 'Hey Kato,' he said. His hair was wild; he looked scrambled.

She clutched at the front of his shirt.

He laughed. 'Everything okay? We've seen you with an assortment of gentlemen, but that's nothing new.'

'I don't—' Keteki said toddlerishly.

He smiled down at her. 'You don't?'

She laughed and shook her head. 'I don't want to. When can we go home?'

'But it's the lock-in now, Kato. What about your new friends?' Tom asked. 'For example, the musician. He looks very Byronic.'

Keteki laughed, but didn't let go of Tom's shirt. 'What were you and Elsa having that serious conversation about? I could hear bits of it in that strange room.'

Tom disengaged his shirt gently. 'If you could hear, why are you asking?' he said, but he'd stopped smiling. 'Relax, Kato. Have another drink.' His eyes were clouded.

A further hubbub rose from the whettle room. 'Let's see what's happening,' Tom said. He put a hand on Keteki's shoulder, then let it go.

The back room was dense with smoke and voices. Around fifteen people stood a little to the right of the door.

Keteki paused. 'What's going on?' she said. She touched an elbow, which turned out to be Pete's. 'Where's Elsa?' she asked, for want of knowing what to say.

'Probably wherever Tom is,' Pete said.

Keteki looked at her shoes. In the middle of the knot of people, Neil's voice broke out. 'Well, but why don't you just listen to the fecking music?'

A deeper, angry voice, very English. 'I fail to see why someone who's just passing through the pub in my family's village should tell me how to behave, in the whettle room of all places.'

A younger voice. 'Geraint, we're all tired. Let's calm down.'

'Fuck off, Albert.'

Keteki sighed. She touched Pete's elbow again. 'I'm going to the bar. Do you want a drink?'

Pete shook his head. 'I've had enough.'

'Okay,' Keteki said. She edged out of the crowd, and could hear Neil saying plaintively, 'I just wanted to try out some new material. It's influenced by...'

Jonathan was in the front bar. He had a corner table and perked up when he saw her. 'Ketecky!'

She paused, wondering if it was a simple fact that life was better in a place where people pronounced your name properly. Briefly but authentically she missed Ved.

'Where's your son?' she asked Jonathan.

'Who?'

'The boy you arrived with?'

'Oh, Andrew. My nephew. Staying with me. Bit of a problem child, in all honesty.'

'I'm going to the bar,' Keteki said. The man behind it was courtly, with impressively curved sideburns. He inclined his large head towards her.

'Could I have some of that lovely whisky?' she said. 'It might be an Islay malt. A new friend—tall, like you—he bought it an hour ago.'

'I know the one you mean. Richard Kerrigan?'

'Yes,' she said.

'He's a good man,' said the landlord.

There were screeches and cheers from the back room. Keteki turned her head, but the landlord seemed unperturbed.

'How many whiskies for you, young lady?'

'Two, I suppose.' She sighed and glanced at Jonathan over her shoulder. He was slumped, staring at his phone.

'Friend of yours?' inquired the landlord.

'He came here in a rowing boat,' said Keteki in wonder.

'That's our skiff,' said the landlord. 'Thaddeus Miller. This is my pub.'

'Keteki Sharma,' she said, and held out her hand. 'Er, I met a gentleman earlier who cuts reeds,' she said.

'Ian Swanton,' said Thaddeus. 'The Swantons are all a little eccentric.'

Keteki giggled. 'The man over there,' she said. 'He broke

my heart when I was nineteen. I haven't seen him in twenty years.'

'You don't look old enough for any of this to be true,' Thaddeus said.

Keteki smiled. 'You're flattering me,' she said. 'It's true I can't quite believe it happened.'

Thaddeus shot Jonathan a look. 'No more can I,' he said.

'I wonder what he's doing here,' Keteki said.

The strains of the last, least interesting song from Neil's set, 'And I'll be seeing you again,' broke from the back room.

'Can I ask you something?' Keteki said. She felt a tipsy kinship with the massive landlord, a person who, like her, seemed untied to anyone else.

'Anything you like, my beautiful young duchess.'

'What *is* a whettle?'

Thaddeus smiled. 'It's a bit of a disgraceful Suffolk story, in truth,' he said. 'But I can tell you that this part of Suffolk has always been a bit of a haven for smugglers. We're out of the way, but on the water. That's how they used to bring in their stuff to avoid the customs men.'

'What were they smuggling?' Keteki asked.

'Rum and tea mostly, I think,' said the landlord.

'Tea—we grow that in my place,' she was beginning when Jonathan bellowed from the corner, 'Ketecky!'

Keteki sighed and nodded to Thaddeus. She went back to the table and handed Jonathan a glass. 'So,' she said only a little ironically, 'how have you been?'

'Thanks,' he said heavily. 'Now, did you know Janine? I've forgotten.'

Keteki grinned. As far as she remembered, Janine was the girl he'd been with directly after her. 'No,' she said.

'Well, we were together for ages. But, disaster.' He shook his head like a wet dog.

'Disaster for ages?' murmured Keteki.

'Two little girls,' said Jonathan. 'I hope they don't turn out like her.' He continued to talk for some time, while Keteki zoned out, sometimes saying 'Mm,' and 'Really?'

'It's exhausting,' Jonathan concluded, some time later. Keteki could not but agree. Ved, she reflected, was probably also flirting with some woman somewhere. She examined Jonathan. How like life to bring him back when she no longer had any interest in finding out why he'd left her. People just did things.

The phone in her pocket buzzed. It was a message from Ved. 'Please reply,' he said shamelessly.

'Do you spend a lot of time,' Keteki asked Jonathan, 'thinking about things from other people's point of view?'

'I'm not sure what you mean,' Jonathan said cautiously.

'You know. Do you imagine what other people think? Your wife, your children. Your nephew. Where is he, by the way?'

'God knows,' Jonathan said. 'Probably looking depressed in a corner. Teenagers are impenetrable. Ket-ecky, it's so lovely to see you.' He stroked her wrist. 'We should have dinner some time.'

Keteki smiled and looked into her glass, where a small mouthful of whisky remained. Since the lock-in, the lights had dimmed in the front bar. In the other corner, two black-jacketed men were deep in a sombre conversation like figures in a Cézanne painting. Behind the bar, Thaddeus was in shadow, but the darkness around him seemed warm.

'Why did you come here?' she said abruptly.

'My brother has a house nearby. King's Bletchley. Um, give me a minute. Just need a slash.' He lumbered up, and Keteki slipped out of the front door. The garden was cool, but after a while she walked round to the mill pond. She took off her shoes and sat on the grass, the creak of the wheel and the rushing water replacing thoughts.

A while later, there were footsteps, and a herbal scent. She opened her eyes and yawned.

'Hi, sorry, would it be all right,' a young voice asked politely, 'for me to smoke here?'

'Sure.'

'Thanks.' He sat a few feet away. After a puff, he said, 'Did you want any … it's weed.'

'I noticed,' Keteki said. 'No thanks.'

'No one ever wants to smoke, I shouldn't have asked,' the youth mumbled.

'It's nice that you asked,' Keteki said.

'I smoke a lot now,' the young man said. He edged closer.

'Oh,' Keteki said. 'You're Jonathan's nephew.'

'Yes, did you meet him?'

'I used to know him in Oxford,' she said. 'In fact we—well, it was before he was with his wife. He kind of dumped me.' She chuckled.

'I wouldn't worry,' said Andrew. 'They're miserable.'

'Yes, he did mention that.'

'But so is everyone. The system seems fucked. Are you sure you don't want some?'

'Okay,' said Keteki. She accepted the joint and took a puff, then held it in as seriously as if she were doing a breathing exercise. She exhaled and took another puff. 'That's a lot stronger than I'm used to.'

Andrew finished the joint. 'I'd better go and find Jonathan.'

When Keteki went back inside, Thaddeus, the Green Knights, Ian the rushcutter and Neil were all at a table with high-backed benches. Everyone seemed to have been drinking dedicatedly for a while.

'But folk music,' the tallest, angriest Green Knight was saying. 'It's not exactly for today, is it?'

'No no no,' the Irish singer said. 'You don't understand. Folk music isn't from yesteryear. It's from now. It's from any time, including the future, including today, including tomorrow.'

'Can you explain that?' said the landlord, inclining his enormous head towards Neil.

'Well, it's like, there might be a nightingale and a fair maid in a song, but there might also be a trip to Penney's. I mean, Primark. And a spaceman.'

'Isn't that more like pop?' asked another Green Knight with red hair.

'You've an erroneous conception of—Keteki!' said Neil, jumping up. He had knocked over two glasses. 'Oh feck.'

'You idiot,' said Geraint, the angry Knight. He stood up, dripping.

Thaddeus rose. He was wider than a door, it seemed, and stouter than oak. 'Albert,' he said, 'go and get a cloth. We're all going to remain calm like the good friends we are.' And he reseated Geraint by the simple method of pressing down on his shoulder as on a button that had mistakenly sprung up. Albert hurried off, and the other Knights stood back from the wet table. Keteki returned to the corridor in search of Pete, half thinking it might be a good idea to find him before he ran into Tom and Elsa.

In the now quiet, shadowy whettle room, Pete was at a table with Richard Kerrigan and the two young women from the bathroom.

'Hey,' said Pete, looking relaxed.

'Hey,' said Keteki. Richard Kerrigan was telling a story. When he finished, both the girls, Lisa and Katie, laughed a lot. A shadow moved out of the corner, the dog from earlier. He left the room.

'I'm really tired,' Keteki said to Pete.

'Find everyone,' Pete said. 'Maybe Tom's sober enough to drive.'

Keteki sighed. 'Oh. I forgot there'd be no question of a taxi.' Pete rolled his eyes. 'I'll ask the landlord,' she said.

In the front bar, Jonathan Carlisle was asleep, head on the table. The dog lay on the bar and looked at her with intelligent eyes.

'Can I get a whisky and ginger?' Keteki asked.

The dog looked deprecating and crossed his paws.

'I know,' Keteki said. 'Taps can't be easy.'

His tail began to thump.

Keteki found Thaddeus in the side bar, peacefully chatting to the Knights. 'Yes, my lovely lass?' he said.

'I'm sorry to bother you, Thaddeus,' she said. She sat on the arm of the settle and rested a palm on his massive shoulder. 'I'm just really tired.'

'Aye, it's late enough.'

'I'm not sure what to do about getting home.'

'To the Hursts'?'

'Yes. I can get into the house, but we seem to be missing two people.'

Thaddeus sucked in his lower lip. His face looked like one of the presidents' heads at Mount Rushmore. 'Albert will take you in the skiff, and then the van,' he said. 'And Argus will go with you.'

'Who?' said Keteki.

Albert smiled. 'The dog.'

'When do you want to go, maid? Ah, she's already asleep.'

Keteki nodded. The world was swimming. She thought of her rooms in Guwahati, in Delhi, realised with surprise she wasn't in either of those places, wondered what her aunt was up to, thought of eating rice, felt a vague sadness. In her pocket, her phone began to buzz. She took it out and saw with some surprise that it was Ved. On the third ring, the battery died.

'Albert,' said Thaddeus.

'I'm ready,' Albert said. 'Can you bring Argus to the front?'

Keteki followed them to the front bar. Thaddeus held Argus's collar and bent to speak into the dog's ear. Then he moved back, and Argus got to his feet and poured himself off the bar, landing lightly on the floor. Keteki felt she was both floating and drowning in the surface of things. Thaddeus held open the door, and Keteki, Albert and Argus went out. The darkness was loamy: it was like Guinness, chocolate mousse, velvet.

Albert followed the dog into the skiff. Keteki turned. Thaddeus stood, huge and reassuring, at the end of the land. 'Thank you for coming to the Rushcutters,' he said.

'I loved it,' Keteki said. She put up her arms and hugged him.

'Albert and Argus will see you home,' he said. 'Sleep well.'

Trees massed over the river, and the sky was made of thought and hope. The water was inky, distressing. Albert talked, a Page of Optimism: she couldn't understand the signs he used, the words, if that is what they were, but he kept up a stream of remarks, and Keteki, to her own bemusement, heard someone with a clear yet husky voice respond.

She felt a bump in her lower back. The boat had docked. Argus got out first, then Albert tied up the boat, got out and helped Keteki. There was soft damp grass and the metal of a van door, the sound of an engine and a moment before that, or perhaps years earlier, Albert's voice saying, 'Did you say there was a key?'

'Last but one in the dogfeed,' said Keteki. She gestured at the greenhouse and sat down in the gravel of the drive.

Centuries passed, the Romans, the Visigoths, the Dark Ages, the Renaissance, the Ahoms, Xonkordeb, the Burmese invasion, the British. If there could only be bedding into which to put her face. But the back door was opened, Albert said something about her friends, Keteki said yes, Argus's warm, intelligent eyes telegraphed a message to Dexter, who was barking at the door, and she was up the stairs. The darkness folded in. As Keteki fell into sleep, she heard her own body letting out strange moans of relief.

'Are you sure you can't just drive back early tomorrow morning? That's what we're doing,' she said, though the car was packed and Pete and Elsa were leaving.

'Work,' said Elsa, and shrugged. She looked tired, but younger somehow because of the shadows under her eyes.

Keteki hugged them. She and Tom watched their car out of the drive. Back in the kitchen, under the gaze of the rushcutters in the tapestry, she helped Tom tidy. Things went in the recycling bin and the food bin; they loaded the dishwasher, scraped plates, rinsed dishes, screwed the tops of jars back on, squirted cleaning spray, wiped surfaces. Keteki swept the kitchen floor. Tom mopped it. They sat on the sofa, exhausted, with the second half of a bottle of red wine.

'Let's take a look at the headlines,' Tom said. He reached for the remote and turned on the television, to Keteki's silent horror. She leaned back, still immersed in the chemical scent of the kitchen cleaner and the memory of the food crud she'd collected from the floor.

'The tidying up …' she said.

'I know, the rest of the house is a mess,' Tom said, and yawned. 'But I'll be coming and going, so I'll deal with it later.'

Keteki looked at him sideways. 'So, you and Elsa,' she said.

Tom sighed. 'I know. Fucking stupid. The only thing I can say is that, since Laura and I broke up, I've just been living a life without rules. But Elsa suddenly thought she might be pregnant, and we both freaked out. This morning she got her period.'

'Whew!' Keteki raised an eyebrow.

'Phew indeed.' Tom grinned. 'And what's the exciting news in your love life?'

'I think it's kind of the opposite. I've never really had any rules, but I'm getting bored of it. It sounds like complete freedom.' She picked at the cushion on her lap. 'But it's another kind of rut.'

Tom smiled, and his crows' feet came out. 'Thinking of settling down?' he enquired.

'No, God, no. Well. Maybe.' They both laughed.

'Who's the guy?' Tom asked.

'He's English, but Indian. Ved. Does something in finance. He works for a company that invests in other companies, or something. He's like a consultant.'

'Huh. Good guy?'

'I've no idea,' Keteki said. 'We've been spending more time together in the last six weeks. It seems like it's easy for us to be around each other. But I don't know what he … if he …'

Tom chuckled. 'You sound positively human, Kato. I guess even you had to face some challenges eventually.'

'I've faced plenty, thanks,' she said.

'Tell me more about … Ved?' Tom patted her knee with the remote.

Keteki sighed and hugged her cushion. 'We met at the airport last year. He was on his way to India. Weirdly enough, the lighting company he was on his way to see is the one I've been working on the exhibition for.' She paused. 'When Ved and I first met, we briefly … I mean, I didn't think anything of it.'

'No, well,' said Tom drily.

'I wasn't looking for anything,' Keteki said. 'But we kept in touch. Then he came to Assam, but I wasn't sure, and now I'm in England and I don't know what he thinks.'

Tom laughed. 'Hang on, Kato. I want to change the channel. Then I can concentrate.' He fiddled with the remote. 'Hm, *One Born Every Minute* … *Posh Pets* … oh fuck it, let's have the cricket replay. All right. Now,' and he turned to a slightly affronted Keteki. 'Have you talked to him about this?'

'Ved? No. Wouldn't he have asked if he wanted to be with me?'

'Not necessarily,' Tom said. 'He might not know what you want.'

Keteki sighed.

'It's a conversation,' Tom said. 'Find out.'

The next morning at eight o'clock, as they drove past the furniture and carpet warehouses of the North Circular, Keteki looked for the Everlasting Lucifer hot air balloon. But she didn't see it. The city was upon them, grey, various, profuse, and Mark was phoning her.

'Hello?' she answered.

18

The dark

'THE RAIN,' VED said. 'I mean, obviously people talk about it.' He looked out of the window. 'I just wasn't expecting quite this.'

'Yes, yes, Ved,' said Joy mama. 'We have rain. And storms.' He wandered towards the bookshelves, taking with him one of the storm lanterns. The room was otherwise in darkness, except when lightning flashed, and was followed by an enormous clap of thunder. Absurd volumes of water were pouring out of the sky.

Ved flinched. 'It sounds like the end of the world,' he said. 'Like the sky is cracking open.'

Joy mama looked at Ved, and the younger man thought he smiled. But Joy mama turned back to the bookshelf. 'I was looking for two things,' he said. 'Some photographs of Ketu as a child, her mother, me, our family. And another thing, a book of proverbs, quite interesting.'

'When did your sister pass away?' Ved said.

There was a cough. 'Ved, I'm not sure I got your meaning.'

'Sorry,' Ved said. 'I mean, when did she die? Maybe you'd rather not talk about it though.'

The lamp in the older man's hand bobbed its way back to the table. Joy mama sat down, and the lamp joined its fellow. 'Ved,' said Joy mama. 'Forgive a terribly old-fashioned question, but what *are* your intentions towards my niece?'

'Long term,' Ved said. 'Long long-term. If she'll have me. I don't think I've been that clear about it till now. Everything happened quite fast.'

Joy mama nodded. 'I have mentioned this, I think, but she comes from a ruptured background. My sister is not an easy person. Can be delightful, when she wants to be.' He smiled. 'Her husband—my brother-in-law, rest his soul—came from a very good family. They were a brilliant couple at first. He was good-looking, intelligent, just starting in the tea trade. But he liked a drink.'

'They only had one child?' Ved asked.

Joy mama nodded. 'My sister lost a child before Ketu was born. But afterwards, my brother-in-law was travelling, my sister was in Guwahati, and Ketu was sent between her aunt and here. Things went wrong.' He wiped an eye. 'Terribly wrong. The family has let Ketu down. She was sent to boarding school. It was the best thing to do, but it was hard. She was only seven years old.'

Ved nodded.

'Mother and daughter are not close, Ved. My sister doesn't keep in touch. She moved to Dimapur quite some time back, and lives with a gentleman there.' There was a flash of lightning.

'Hang on,' said Ved. 'Keteki's mother's not dead?'

Joy mama stared at him. 'Not at all.'

The thunder cracked hugely and wind made the trees thrash.

'This is a strange country,' Joy mama said.

'India?'

'Assam. So beautiful, yet always being unmade. Earthquakes, floods, such fertile land. The river, of course. I wonder when the power will come back.'

'To Assam?' said Ved.

'The electricity, Ved. If it doesn't return soon, the best thing is for us to eat and go to bed. Look at that.' A flying cockroach battered itself against the glass of the storm lamp. Joy mama tutted and flicked it off, but not for long. 'We can go to the kitchen,' he said. 'The inverter only works in some rooms. So you haven't talked to Ketu? About your plans, or hopes?' he added, leading the way down the passage. They crossed the dining room and went through the door into the kitchen, which was lit with a gentle glow.

'Is that a Lucifer?' Ved asked.

'Could be,' said Joy mama. 'They give a pleasant light. It's running off the inverter.'

Tuku sat at the table, reading the newspaper. He looked up and said, 'O, Dada,' and smiled.

Joy mama issued a series of coaxing instructions, patted Tuku on the shoulder, sighed and said, 'Bade, we'll eat in here. Do sit down.'

As they did, Joy mama added, 'One thing about you does remind me of Ketu. A quality of not being quite at home. Did you go to boarding school too?'

Ved shook his head. 'No,' he said. 'Lived at home till I went to university. But maybe moving from India to England when I was a child, or the kind of school I went to, had something to do with it. It's true, there's no one place ...' He thought of his flat and felt a sense of respite, but not welcome. Although in the last few weeks, when Keteki had been there often, he'd begun to notice how good it felt to be at home with her.

'Would you like something to drink, Ved? A beer?'

'Sure,' Ved said.

Tuku brought a bottle, beaded with moisture. Joy mama poured two glasses, handed one to Ved, and clinked it with his own.

'Won't you join us?' Ved asked Tuku, who smiled and waved a hand.

'I don't drink beer,' he explained. 'But please enjoy.'

'Oh!'

'And Ketu,' said Joy mama. 'Do you think she'll say yes?'

'To what?' said Ved, losing track for a minute. He corrected himself quickly. 'I haven't had a chance to think things through. I need to figure out what to say, or ask.'

Joy mama raised an eyebrow. 'Yes, it does seem as though deciding that would be a good idea,' he said drily.

'In your life,' Ved said. 'Have you felt that … you knew what to do? For the future? And then, later, felt that you'd done the right thing?'

The older man laughed hard, then extended a large paw. 'Sorry, sorry Ved,' he said. 'I'm afraid wisdom hasn't yet descended. I'm not sure it will. I resisted some things, including having a family, because I couldn't tell how the future would be for me. And yet,' he smiled, looking down at the palm of his hand, 'for the most part, I've lived a quiet life, in the house where I was born. There are elements of my existence that remain private even from those closest to me, it's true.' He looked Ved in the eye. 'But that is true of everyone, is it not?'

Ved felt behind his collar. After a pause, he wondered,

'Does anyone really decide what to do? Or is it just periods of lethargy alternating with spasms of action?'

Joy mama laughed. 'That's well put, Ved. I don't know. In my case, there have been long periods of contentment.' He stretched out his arms, and did something yogic looking behind his back, apparently stretching each shoulder. 'The more I sat still, you know, figuratively speaking, the happier I was.'

Ved leaned on his elbows, hunched his shoulders and drank his beer. He watched Tuku move around the kitchen, loose-limbed but compact, and envied his grace. The inimitably sweet smell of mustard oil, heated till it smoked, filled the room.

Joy mama gave Ved an amused look, but didn't offer a penny for his thoughts. Ved went on sipping his beer and imagining different futures with Keteki. In one, wearing slightly Seventies clothing, they smilingly looked after two small children. He realised he'd conflated childhood memories and his crush on Katharine Ross in *The Graduate*. In another image, he and Keteki fought constantly, but sometimes had incandescent sex. In a third, he saw himself in an airport lounge, disconsolate. Was he waiting for her? Or going away? He didn't even know which future to hope for.

'I worry,' he said. 'I worry about making mistakes.'

'In one view,' said Joy mama, 'there is no such thing as a mistake. Of course, that's a fairly rarefied way of looking at things.'

'My work,' said Ved. He finished his beer. On the stove, fish was frying, making delectable smells. 'It's mysterious,' Ved went on. 'The Lucifers—it was all going so well. But now these defects. The testing seemed to have been done properly, it was checked. I don't understand how this could have happened.'

'I suppose these things aren't uncommon,' said Joy mama. 'There was that new car a few years ago. Some of the engines exploded.'

Ved nodded. 'It almost seems as though someone or something doesn't want the Lucifer to succeed,' he said. 'There was that factory fire. Maybe I'm just being superstitious.'

'Well, people have their reasons to be disgruntled,' Joy mama said. There was an almighty crack of thunder, a howl of wind, and the lights went out.

'The inverter has blown,' said Tuku.

'Oh,' said Ved.

'We do have candles, of course.' Joy mama said something to Tuku, who acquiesced and went off.

Ved looked at the moving shadows from the door into the dining room. He had a sense of the house behind its daytime appearance. In the dark, physical objects became inquisitive presences, inviting him to look beneath the surface. He had a sudden image of his mother, sitting on the gold-coloured velour sofa in a friend's house in Hounslow, talking about Ved. 'He swears like a trooper,' she'd said, not without pride. That was a daylight image. The night-time one was different: thumps from his parents' bedroom, the sound of his mother's voice like broken glass, berating Ved's father, Ved clutching his duvet, and later wanking into tissues while he thought about the breasts and arses of the girls he'd stared at that day.

There was light again; Tuku returned with the storm lanterns. Outside, there were cracks of breaking wood. 'The trees,' said Joy mama sadly.

'Keteki,' said Ved.

Her uncle, quizzical and refined, looked enquiring.

'She never talks about her parents but I'm fairly sure she said her mother ...' Ved paused, and thought about it. 'Maybe it was just implied by the past tense,' he said.

The older man exhaled. 'If you'd seen Ketu as a child,' he said. 'Round-faced, curious, loving little girl. But things were not good around her. My sister,' he sighed, 'is spoiled. She was the baby of the family. My brother-in-law began by being very in love with her, but it became exhausting to try to please someone who refused to be pleased. And it was easy for him to find other women.' He shrugged. 'We are old-fashioned in Assam. The family counts for more than an ideal of romantic love.'

Tuku came to say dinner was ready. He brought to the table a fish curry, dal, rice and a dish of greens.

'You'll like these, Ved,' said Joy mama. Tuku sat with them and ate with his hand. Joy mama and Ved used forks. As the meal ended, the overhead light came back on.

'Oh good,' said Joy mama. It was still raining, but calmly now, like rain in another place. A couple of enormous cockroaches ran around on the floor. Tuku, tutting, went to hit them on the head and throw them out of the door. Joy mama put away the leftovers, and Ved and Tuku tidied up.

'It's nice of you to remember us, Ved,' said Joy mama. He, Ved, and Tuku sat on the little sofa in the front room. The television was on. 'Where are you off to tomorrow?'

'I'm going to Bombay,' said Ved. 'I fly out from there at night. But before that, I need to meet Mr Ganesh and figure out what to do next. I've been to both factories, I've seen all the reports. I wanted—'

He stopped, because in the break from the Assamese news, a familiar ad had begun. A boy was studying at a table in a harshly lit room. Next door, a husband and wife quarrelled. Suddenly, the cricketer Mahendra Singh Dhoni appeared. 'Need more light in your life?' he asked, dubbed into Assamese. The voiceover said, 'Ebherlasting Lucifer,' and the little boy at the table came back into shot, now studying happily in a golden glow. The couple in the next room smiled at each other, the husband stroking the wife's hair. The scenes were nearly the same as before, but everything was different. 'Everlasting Lucifer,' said the voiceover. 'Lasting happiness.'

'Lovely advertisement, Ved,' said Joy mama.

'Thanks,' Ved said. 'I don't know if maybe we should have waited. Er, can I talk to you?'

Tuku began to get up, but Joy mama shook his head. 'We can go to my room, Ved,' he said.

It was small and bare, with two chairs, a table, a bed and a framed photo of a man in white with a halo.

'Sit down, Ved,' said Joy mama. He indicated the armchair, and scooped up a sweater and one of the cats, who gave Ved a dirty look and jumped onto the bed.

'Um,' said Ved. 'I've been thinking about it, and I want to ask Keteki to marry me.'

Her uncle regarded him. 'You've been thinking about it since dinner?'

'I want to make a life with her,' Ved said.

'But you don't know each other that well, do you?' Joy mama folded his arms. 'Forgive me. I want her to be happy.'

'You don't think I'm the man for the job?'

The older man smiled. 'Is it man's work? I'd be glad to see her with someone, and happy, I know that. I just don't know if everyone is meant to live with other people.'

'Can you tell me more about that?' Ved said.

'Wouldn't it be better to talk to Ketu?'

'She doesn't talk about everything.'

'Well,' said her uncle. 'Perhaps she doesn't wish to.'

Ved nodded. Then, 'Do—do you think there's anyone else?' he asked, and fixed his eyes on Joy mama.

'No idea, Ved. I mean, there must be countless people, but I'm not aware of anything serious. I'm not going to tell tales, but I do want to help you. I just don't know if you have what it takes.' He removed his glasses and rubbed his eyes.

'What will it take?' asked Ved.

'Patience.'

'I can be patient,' Ved said.

Keteki's uncle sighed. 'The trying thing about patience is that you have to find it just when you can't take things anymore.' He opened his hands, palms up. 'I'll tell you the secret, Ved. Let people be who they are and love them as they are.'

'How would you say Keteki is?' said Ved.

Her uncle smiled, the secretive line near his eyes appearing. 'I wouldn't like to try to fix her,' he said, 'like a butterfly with a pin. But there is something very joyful in her.'

'Yes,' said Ved.

'But also a sadness that's too much for someone so young. She's seen the worst of human nature. I sometimes feel if she had a stable home she could do anything.'

'I'd like to give her that,' Ved said. He felt warm in his chest, but also a pang of self-doubt: Stability? You?

'People who have lived through difficult times are not always easy, Ved,' said Joy mama. He rose. 'But I should stop talking, I feel I've said enough. It's late, let's sleep. Do you have everything you need?'

'Yes,' Ved said. He stood too. 'Thank you so much. You've been so kind, I really—'

'Goodnight, Ved,' said Joy mama. He patted the other man's shoulder and raised a hand in farewell as he turned on the bathroom light.

In Bombay, Ved went to his hotel, a tall tower in the middle of the city. He phoned Ganesh, who said he would meet him there. An hour later, there was a knock at Ved's door. Ganesh was in shirtsleeves and looked tired.

They sat at a table and chairs near the window. Outside, Ved looked down on rows of tenement buildings with balconies, then an open space, a Victorian industrial chimney, a crane. The last remains of the mill lands were being swallowed into luxury apartments, malls and hotels.

Ved poured two glasses of water, and passed one to Ganesh. 'The popping bulbs,' he said. 'What's going on? The figure for refunds is too high. We reviewed the manufacturing and testing, there doesn't seem to be anything there. How is this happening?' He picked up a sheaf of printouts. 'And these online reviews. I know some of them are ridiculous. But people are talking about how the bulbs grow brighter in certain situations? Around certain people, even, and then dim around other people. That's got to be because of something like voltage fluctuations?'

Ganesh didn't answer.

Ved went on, 'You must have seen some of this. Anand V. from Pune says on some site called Quora that the bulb always dims around his mother-in-law, who complains a lot.

Someone else has a story, presumably apocryphal, about a political party meeting in a hall lit with Lucifers, where the bulbs began to fizz and pop. Well?' Ved was irritated. The journey from Jorhat to Dibrugarh had been long, followed by a flight in a tiny plane to Calcutta and a wait in the airport before the flight to Bombay. This whole project was becoming so slippery. 'You don't seem very—' he began sharply, then pulled himself up. He sipped his water.

'I think we should have something better than water,' Ganesh said. He reached into his bag and removed a bottle of whisky. 'Shall we call down for ice and soda?'

After it arrived, Ganesh poured them whiskies. 'Ved,' he said. 'It's not a very coherent story.'

'Go on,' Ved said. 'I didn't have plans for the evening anyway.'

'Well,' Ganesh said, 'bear in mind that when scientific discoveries are made, very often the people who make them were looking for something else. We use the word invention, but the truth is that the new is only revealed to those who are open to working with things as they are. When we developed the filament of the Lucifer, we were looking for a way to make a bulb last a very long time. What we found ...' He stopped to sip his drink. 'You know we call it an intelligent filament. It has its own responsiveness.'

Ved nodded.

'Do you remember the man who worked on the Lucifer? You met him the first time you came to Chennai. Shashidharan.'

'I remember,' Ved said. The retired scientist, thin and ascetic, had a charmingly childlike smile.

'He's not religious,' said Ganesh. 'But when we noticed this property of the Lucifers, after some of us took the first bulbs home to try, he said, "Of course, light becomes brighter when it is really seen."' Ganesh smiled. 'And that's all I've been able to get out of him.'

Ved rubbed his eyes. From seventeen storeys below, he heard car horns honking, and looked down at the city, busy with homegoing traffic, the leaves of old trees heavy with dust, and the streets damp and dirty. 'But,' he said desperately, 'light is measurable, isn't it?'

'In our tests,' Ganesh said, 'the Lucifers respond exactly as one would expect. Of course voltage fluctuation can affect them, but that doesn't account for these reports, or for ...'

Ved remembered the darkness of the sea outside the windows of his suite, that first night with Keteki. 'The way you feel around them,' he said.

Ganesh nodded. Below, Ved heard temple bells and the cries of birds. The air was smoky with twilight.

'And the popping?' he said. 'You didn't expect that either?'

The other man took a sip of his whisky. He swallowed, then shook his head. 'We didn't,' he said. 'But you know, Ved, in our country—' He stopped. 'I must ask that you don't repeat this,' he said.

'I can't promise that,' Ved said. He looked at Ganesh's mute face. 'Okay. Please tell me,' he said.

'These have been dark times,' Ganesh said. 'Not for the first time, certainly. The Seventies, the Emergency. But the climate now ... scientists are hounded. People are attacked even on suspicion of eating beef. There is so much—the word is intolerance, but I don't think that is right. We shouldn't have to tolerate each other. We should let everyone be who he is.'

'And love him for it,' said Ved, echoing Joy mama.

Ganesh smiled. 'I don't think the Constitution goes that far. But it does ask us to let everyone be.'

'Haven't these tensions always existed though?' Ved said.

'Yes, of course. There have been terrible periods in history. I'm not advocating for some kind of abstract saintliness. But the overall atmosphere has changed, now. It's ugly,' Ganesh said. He hunched his shoulders.

'But—the light bulb?' Ved felt he was losing his grip on things.

'Ved, nothing exists in a vacuum,' Ganesh said. 'None of us is in a private universe.'

'No man is an island,' said Ved dully, imagining himself as a godforsaken atoll.

Ganesh smiled. 'None of us thought it would be this extreme.'

'Hang on,' Ved said. 'You thought something might happen?'

The other man eyed him. 'We did notice certain changes in the bulb. But it is after all just a light bulb, Ved.'

'Don't you care about your business?' Ved pleaded.

Ganesh looked him in the eye. 'The Lucifer is a rare and unexpected thing, Ved. I know these events come infrequently. I'm an engineer too, you know, by training. But the world of business isn't what it was in my father's or grandfather's time. I don't know if I want to fit in with the way things seem to have to be done now, and the compromises we would have to make: bribes, courting dignitaries, ministers, celebrities. As you know, we are a family-run firm, and most of the board are our family members, so once I've spoken with them and we have met, I'll let you know how we stand.'

Ved put down his glass. 'I need to talk to my colleagues too,' he said. 'Let's not be rash. I think the best thing—' He became aware that he was tipsy, and feeling nauseous. 'There is an exit agreement, of course, but I never thought ... well, we'll be in touch.' He stood up.

Ganesh stood too. 'Ved, if you're free, come home for dinner. The car is downstairs. After that, I can have you dropped at the airport in good time for your flight.'

'That's very kind,' Ved said.

At the airport, waiting for his severely delayed London flight, Ved drank and texted Keteki. 'Back in London in the morning. In Bombay now. Can you come over? I should be home by ten.'

The message wasn't delivered; neither was a text he sent to her Indian number. He called; both numbers were unreachable.

19

Life changing

VED WENT STRAIGHT to the office. He was coming out of the executive bathroom, having put on one of the new shirts he kept in his bottom desk drawer, his face stinging from aftershave, when he heard, 'Ved Ved!'

Ved turned. It was Graham. 'Hey man,' Ved said.

'Back from …' Graham said.

'India. Bombay.'

'Oh wow! How's it going with that girl?'

'Great,' said Ved automatically. He felt a mild unease.

'And the light bulb?'

'I think it might be going tits up. I'm not sure yet.'

'Really?' Graham followed Ved into his office.

'The guy who owns the company is losing his bottle,' Ved said. 'Things are going wrong with the product even though early sales were good. I can't figure out what's happening. I guess also, it's just been a long time since I've had to abort a project.'

'Aha.' Graham stood inside Ved's office, looking at his books and curios: an enamel inlay box from Tashkent, a marmoset skull from Hong Kong, an antique abacus. In the corner of the office was a box of Lucifers. Ved went to look at it. It was empty.

'What happened to my light bulbs?' Ved said.

Graham laughed. '"What happened to my agent?"' he quoted.

'No, really,' Ved said. 'Where are they?'

'People took them home to try out,' Graham said.

Ved looked up. 'Did you?'

'Yeah.'

'Where did you put it?' Ved asked.

'At home,' Graham said. 'First I tried it in my vintage Anglepoise.'

Ved nodded, and eyed Graham's suit. It had a painting of a Japanese courtesan amorously entangled with a giant squid on the back and left sleeve of the jacket. 'Your jacket,' Ved said. 'Is this a thing now?'

Graham shrugged. 'Scott Souster made it, but I got it painted by a final year student at the Royal College of Art. It's a one-off.'

'Good,' Ved said.

'Anyway, the bulb,' Graham said. 'I'd put it in the Anglepoise, but I don't get around to using the desk that often. So I moved it to the lamp in the hallway. It's a nice, warm light.' He looked confused for a moment. 'I've been having more people over, you know, cooking, and people do seem to get more huggy at the door. It's probably just that the hallway feels warmer or something.'

Ved was opening post at his desk. He found a small silver invitation card. 'What does your day look like, Gray?'

'Shagged,' said Graham cheerfully. 'I've got a late-night conference with an insane Uzbek miner at ten, but he'll probably be super drunk and make me call him back at two in the morning.'

'But the afternoon?' Ved said. 'Want to grab lunch, then check this out quickly?' He passed the card to Graham.

'It *is* free,' said the young man. He looked up, his unlined face an irreproachably blank canvas above his collarless shirt. 'But it's the last day, so they're starting to pack up. It's not a big exhibition, you can get round in twenty minutes before they start dismantling.'

Ved was hurrying towards the door when Graham grabbed his sleeve. 'Look.'

They read an inscription: Natural light, London, today. The skylight let in a watery but resonant light that was very English. Below, there was a high-backed wooden chair for visitors. 'Go ahead, sit down,' Graham said. 'I'm going to wander through.'

Ved sat in the chair. Its wide back cradled him. He looked up, saw nothing in the sky, sat in the light and relaxed, remembering that he was neither in an aeroplane nor about to get on one. Did his thighs look soft? He should go to the gym, or take up martial arts or something. He felt, instead, like curling up like a cat, and purring while Keteki did something nearby: made noise, laughed, clinked in the kitchen, talked on the phone. He closed his eyes.

A few minutes later, he found Graham standing in front of a selection of the vintage Lucifer advertisements. 'Pretty, aren't they?' Graham said.

Ved examined a Mughal-miniature-style depiction of an enormous, many-headed cobra, from whose hoods a tiny light bulb spread radiance over a happy family of homunculi while, outside, a storm raged. 'Yes,' he said. He moved towards the rocking chair next to a standard lamp where a Lucifer glowed. Ved sat in the chair. The light was pretty, sure enough, but his mind twitched. He looked up at the lamp. The bulb bore the correct stamp, and the filament was definitely a Lucifer.

'Did you try the rocking chair?' he asked. Graham was now in front of a display showing the Phiringoti Devi shrine.

'Amazing, a temple to a light bulb, right?' he said, turning to Ved.

'I think any woman can turn into a goddess,' said Ved absent-mindedly. 'Did you sit in the rocking chair though?'

'Uh huh, briefly.'

'How was it?

'The chair?' said Graham, turning to examine it.

'The light.'

Graham blinked, smiled. 'No offence. It didn't particularly do anything for me.' He saw Ved staring. 'Oh hey. I didn't mean ... it's a nice light for sure. Just—'

'Not life-changing?' said Ved slowly.

Graham smiled. 'Maybe life-changing is a bit of an ask for a light bulb?' he suggested.

Ved nodded, stung as a child whose face has been slapped.

20

In the weave

KETEKI SAT ON the wide ledge outside the Millennium Centre in Aizawl and smoked her rollie. The sun shone on her face. Even in the pleather jacket she'd bought yesterday in a street market, she was cold.

She felt a bronchial ache, and inhaled the cold air and traffic fumes along with her cigarette smoke. It was only when she'd landed in Delhi, and was waiting to change planes, that she'd discovered Ved was on his way back to London from Bombay. But the exhibition was done, and she couldn't keep waiting to figure out what was happening. It had been time to go home.

This afternoon, she had her appointment with Kevin Ralte, one of the Aizawl contacts Sunando had given her. 'You don't know Kevin?' Sunando's quiet voice had said with surprise on the phone. 'He does projects with local weavers in Aizawl. You will have seen some of their work in the house. Give him a call, he'll help you.'

A couple of hours later, she walked to the textile department, breathing in the sharp autumnal air. Aizawl felt like another zone, so far east, it was almost in Myanmar. As an Assamese, here she was almost a foreigner, associated more with the mainland than with Mizoram. She looked with interest at the men dressed in dark colours, clustering round street-side noodle stalls, and they and the other Mizo looked at her with curiosity.

'Keteki?' Kevin was tall and softly spoken. He took her into his bare government office. 'Tell me what brings you to Aizawl,' he said.

'I'm interested in starting a handloom project in Assam,' she said. 'I've been doing more design, curating. But I've always wanted to work with textiles. I was thinking of using traditional textile in everyday clothing.'

Kevin nodded, his face wary. 'Like making dresses out of them?'

Keteki smiled. 'I have mixed feelings about it. But I like the idea of those textiles not remaining mainly for special occasions, but also having a voice in everyday life.'

'I make both,' Kevin said. 'Our traditional puan, the wrap-around skirt, and other clothes too. But I'm going to send you to a friend's mother to find out more about the puan.'

Keteki spent a morning in Auntie's immaculate living room, while her host, neatly dressed in a puan, blouse and cardigan, showed her pictures and explained the traditional patterns. 'This one,' pointing to a design of interlinking chevrons, 'we call tiger stripe. This one shows, what do you call it?' She pushed her bifocals up her nose. 'The thing in a field that stops flooding.'

'A dyke?'

'Yes. And this one,' she giggled, 'we call Senior. It's for older ladies.'

Keteki met Kevin at his house for tea and told him what she had been doing. 'I've just been walking around,' she said.

'The light here is incredible. You are east of Assam, and it feels so golden, but also filtered. And you are hill people. This morning, I looked out of the window of my room on the fourth floor of the hotel. I saw a woman on a sloping rooftop across the street. First she hung out some clothes. Then she started sending some messages on her phone, then talking on it, all the while standing on this narrow bit of roof, as though she was inside safely. I could see her standing on one foot, chatting, and with the other foot she was pushing a loose tile.' Keteki burst out laughing. 'I nearly screamed at her to get inside, I thought she would fall.'

Kevin smiled and handed her a cup of green tea.

'I'm noticing the relationship that people have with clothing,' Keteki said. She sat across a little table from him, near his window. 'I've seen the young people, in leather jackets, track pants, running shoes, and the stalls in Zion Street selling sportswear and second-hand clothes, anything and everything.'

'Some of the sportswear will be copies, from Burma,' Kevin said. 'But they are pretty good copies.'

Keteki walked back to the hotel via the Zion Street market as the last light of the dull afternoon faded into smoky evening. She saw straight-haired girls, men in hats, young people in tracksuits, coloured sneakers, sweatshirts, leather and pleather jackets. Everyone moved with toddler-like determination; women bumped into her without apology, sometimes, it seemed, without noticing.

Kevin had promised to take her to meet Mimi, one of the women who wove for him, in the morning. That evening, in her hotel room, Keteki drew: tracksuit pants with a woven tiger stripe down the side, a black shirt whose cuffs folded back to show a geometric pattern in purple, blue, green; a T-shirt with a patterned stripe on the round collar.

On her way to meet Kevin, she stopped at a small bakery for breakfast. Halfway through she picked up her phone. There were some messages from Ved. She dialled a number. When there was an answer, she said, 'Do you know that the place I've seen athletic shoes worn most elegantly was a Buddhist monastery? By the novices. You haven't really seen sportswear till you've seen it on a fourteen-year-old monk.'

There was a dry chuckle on the other end. 'It's perfectly all right, you know, to telephone and begin a conversation like other human beings,' said a deep voice.

'You want me to be like other human beings?' Keteki asked.

'Is it possible?' said Joy mama.

'What do you think,' she said, sipping her very sweet coffee and eyeing the flies around the sugar bowl, 'of the name Social Fabric for a small handloom cooperative?' She took a bite of her very sweet cake and gave up.

Her uncle sighed. 'Are you coming here?' he asked, unusually directly.

'Has something happened?' she said. 'I was going to stay in Aizawl a few more days, then go to Guwahati, then come. It's good to be home.'

'I'm glad,' he said. 'Come when you can.'

'Are you all right?'

'It's not that, Ketu. Tuku's gone.'

'Gone? Gone where?'

'I've no idea.' Her uncle's voice faded back into understatement. 'See you when you get here.'

Abruptly, Keteki wanted to be elsewhere. Aizawl, its smoke and hills, clear air and sunshine and endless churches felt far from home, further from London, her friends, from Mark, from Ved.

She gazed at the line of customers, pointing out different pink and yellow cakes at the counter. Where could Tuku have gone? If he had been a normal housekeeper instead of an unusual family member, they would have assumed he had returned to his village. But he had no village, no family other than them. She thought of Tuku when they were children, a serious but smiling boy, just a year older than Keteki. At the terrible time when a seven-year-old Keteki had been sobbing on her bed, unable to imagine telling anyone what was happening, but also unable to continue, it had been Tuku who had gone to talk to Joy mama. Keteki had been sent away to school. When she returned to Jorhat six months later for her holidays, Sandeep mama was gone. His room was bare; there were gaps on the shelves where his books had been. Joy mama had bent down to her, his face damp. 'You'll never have to see him again,' he said quietly.

At some point in her peripatetic childhood life, Tuku had retreated into the status of a neighbour or a childhood schoolfriend. Her love for him was still there, but she knew less and less about his life. He used to call her bhonti, little sister, but when she became a teenager, began to address her more formally as baideo, older sister.

It was Joy mama who had taken an interest in Tuku, supervised his schooling, enrolled him in junior college and then college. He pushed Tuku to get through college, and he just about graduated before deciding to work for them. He looked after the house, ran errands for Joy mama and made it possible for Keteki to be away without worrying. Tuku said he didn't want to marry or have a family. 'What would Dada do if I were not here?' he asked her smilingly.

She was late to meet Kevin, but half an hour later, they were in a cab, heading to Mimi's house through narrow streets so enclosed by the shape of a hill that they felt like trenches. Keteki looked out at the flowerpots crowded in verandas and balconies, at women leaning down to chat to friends on the street and people on scooters pausing to talk.

By mid-morning, she was eating noodles in Mimi's house. Mimi's daughters and teenage niece wandered around, making tea, watching television, helping their grandmother wind yarn into hanks on a hexagonal frame. Keteki sat on the sofa, near Mimi, who sat on the floor, working on the simple wooden loin loom strapped around her back and braced against her foot. She passed the yarn through the warp threads, then used a heavy wooden shuttle to push it down. She must have felt every movement of the loom against her body, her back straight and her legs stretched out. But she worked quietly, absorbed, smiling when someone spoke to her, but barely looking up even to eat. Each event in the house, every conversation that took place around her seemed to become part of the table runner Mimi was making, so that her mother's animated joking, the talk of her niece and the neighbours who walked through the small house from back to front, or the patter of the older woman selling parathas at the door all became a part of the cloth.

21

Where did he go?

'I DON'T THINK that's a good idea,' said Joy mama.

'I know,' Keteki said. 'I didn't know what else to say.'

'For the police,' said Joy mama, 'Tuku is a servant. If he chooses to leave without saying anything, why would we look for him? Unless he owed us money.' He sighed. 'Whereas in fact,' he went on, 'it is we who owe him everything.'

Joy mama looked thinner and older, but lighter too, like a person about to leave on a journey. Ageing is a broken line, Keteki thought. What did Sandeep mama look like now? She sometimes thought of him—not of the figure who in darkness had terrified her all those years ago, nor the charming, flamboyant uncle she'd adored, but the older man he must be now, some composite of Joy mama's features and her mother's. Did his face show what he had done?

'Tuku didn't say anything about planning to go away?' she asked.

Her uncle shook his head.

'He didn't ask for money?'

'No, not that either. But you know, he must have savings. I made him open a bank account a long time ago, and he didn't really have expenses here. He's not an extravagant person.' Joy mama shrugged.

Keteki hesitated. 'Did you disagree ...'

Her uncle smiled. 'Can you imagine Tuku and I having a quarrel?'

'I haven't known him properly since we were children. How did he spend his time? Who were his friends?'

Her uncle leaned back in his chair. 'He did take leave a few times in the last year. Only a couple of nights at a time. I know that he liked to go to Majuli, he made friends there, in a Mishing village. I thought maybe he also began to visit one of the namghors there.' He smiled. 'He used to borrow my yoga books, you know. I don't know how far he got, we didn't talk about it much. He's a private person. But he's also our family.' He opened the palm of his hand, closed it, then opened it again, fingers splayed, as though the tiniest of birds had flown away. There were tears in his eyes.

That night, on the narrow bed in the room where she slept, Keteki lay and thought about Tuku leaving the house with only a backpack. She saw his gentle smile and smiled herself. Did he have a man, a woman somewhere? His whole life had been lived in their midst, but he remained obscure to them.

Before she turned out the lamp, she looked at the bookshelf where she'd put a bundle of handloom cloth and cotton jersey she'd bought in Aizawl. This time, she mustn't let the energy behind the idea dissipate. She should ... and she turned out the light and fell asleep watching lurid images from folk tales, Tuku's head turning into a fox, a duck, a trickster, a ghost.

22

Rabbit hole

'CAN I COME to see you this weekend?' Ved said.

There was a pause. 'Ved, don't come this weekend,' Keteki said.

'How do you mean, "Don't come"?' said Ved. 'That's not very Assamese.'

He heard her laugh at the other end of the phone. 'I suppose you're right. Joy mama would be horrified. In fact, that's an idea, Ved. Go and see him. I'm sure he'd enjoy the company.'

Ved looked between the railings of his tiny balcony at the tree outside. It was bright with red flowers. The morning was hot and humid, the sky cloudless, and insects buzzed around the leaves. 'But I wanted to come and see you,' he said.

'I'll be working most of the time,' Keteki said. 'The rest of the time, all I want to do is get my clothes washed and maybe sit down and look at a tree for half an hour.'

'I'm looking at a tree now,' said Ved. A crow cawed loudly.

'Sounds like it,' said Keteki, her voice becoming fainter, as though she was already melting away.

'I could come and look at a tree with you,' said Ved.

'Go to Jorhat,' Keteki said. 'You'll have a lovely time.'

'Now that was more of an Assamese no,' he said.

She chuckled. 'Ved, you're fitting in so *well*.'

'Bye,' said Ved sadly and hung up. The balcony was dirty; Guwahati's humidity attracted dust and red earth, which collected daily on windowsills, and in the corners of rooms.

Every morning, his maid came to clean. She burst into the flat any time after six, pushed past a somnolent, indignant Ved at the front door, and tackled the dust. She was small and dishevelled, her hair scraped back anyhow. He'd tried to talk to her in his starter Assamese, and then in Hindi. She gave him a suspicious look and barged past him to the balcony, where she kept the long-tailed broom.

He went back inside and looked around the clean flat. If Keteki wouldn't see him this weekend, he could use some time to get online and check out small ads for second-hand furniture. The previous week, Ved's landlord had dropped in and stood looking round the empty living room. 'Are you planning to buy any furniture?' he'd asked. 'You aren't leaving?'

Ved wasn't leaving. He had a bed, solid teak, bought from a young woman whom he met just after she returned from the gym. Clad in Lycra, she told Ved she was buying a new bed, and smiled at him in a way that made him wonder exactly what was on offer besides the bed. Flirtation was such a routine part of conversation here, surely it couldn't be that simple?

'Well,' said Joy mama that weekend, 'I suppose it's a relic of the way our society was earlier. We do have a different attitude to sex than in the mainland. The Victorians, you know, Ved. They warped this country.'

It was the first time Ved had seen Joy mama in months; the first time since he had left his job, handed the keys of his London flat over to a letting agent and made his way to Guwahati. The older man looked the same, but different. His hair was more silver, and he had cropped it short. He ran a palm over it and smiled at Ved. 'I put you in Ketu's room,' he said. 'It's been used more recently. I've let some parts of the house go a little, I'm afraid.'

Ved nodded, and let himself into the room, where a small ball of fluff was settled on the bed. Pingala. 'Hi there,' he said, offering a finger which the orange cat gently bit.

He put down his bag, washed his hands, and went back to the kitchen to find Joy mama. 'Come, Ved,' he said. He'd made tea and sandwiches. 'We'll eat properly in the evening,' he said. 'I thought you might want something after the train.' Ved sat down and looked round the kitchen. A cap that Tuku used to wear still hung on the back of the door.

'You're looking at Tuku's hat,' said Joy mama. The lines near his mouth were more apparent, a man moving into old age. 'I cut a sad figure, I suppose,' he observed.

'No,' said Ved.

'But also, yes,' said Joy mama. He smiled. 'Don't be alarmed. I'm not feeling particularly sorry for myself right now. The fact is that I've been willing to slip off the scene for much of the time I've found myself on it. Although,' and he gave a throaty chuckle, 'as you will have noticed, I rather like the limelight.'

Ved smiled, felt his eyes prickle and put out his hand to grasp Keteki's uncle's shoulder.

Joy mama bowed his head. 'Thank you, Ved.'

'I'm sure you'll hear from him.'

'As long as he's all *right*, Ved,' said Joy mama. 'That's what matters.' He took off his spectacles and wiped his eyes. 'Anyway,' he said, and smiled. 'Tell me about yourself.

We haven't met since you arrived, I should say returned to Assam. How long has it been, almost three months?' His eyes twinkled. 'Ketu said you had found an apartment?'

'In Uzan Bazar,' Ved said. 'Near the market.'

Joy mama nodded. 'It's the oldest residential area in Guwahati. I am not all that fond of Guwahati, but that is the best place to live. So close to the river. Do you go for walks on the riverside?'

'Sometimes,' Ved said. 'I like those lanes near the river, the old houses.'

'And what else do you do with your days?' Joy mama asked.

'I have some savings,' Ved said, 'from the last twenty years of working. And I have my flat in London, which is rented out to tenants at the moment. So I'm free to take a break. I was hoping,' he said, looked away, then back at Joy mama, 'to make a go of things with Keteki. I thought, instead of expecting her to uproot herself, why not spend some time here, begin learning Assamese, try to experience her world. But I haven't been able to spend much time with her since I arrived.'

It was only about three in the afternoon. But already the old kitchen, it seemed, was growing dimmer and colder as the winter afternoon faded.

Joy mama leaned back in his chair. 'She's absorbed in this thing she's started—she calls it Social Fabric,' he said, with a chuckle. 'I like it, Ved. For the first time, she has something she can put her energy into. I was dubious at first, I'll be honest,' he said, leaning forward and pushing his glasses up his nose. 'But the more I hear, the better it sounds. I think there are around eight women working with her in that village? I understand some are sewing, some are weaving fresh cloth. I don't know exactly what they're making—'

'Oh, it's really exciting,' Ved said. 'They're using the handloom as an element in some really nice basics. T-shirts, track pants, shorts, things that people all over the world would wear. I know the traditional clothes are beautiful in their own right. But I think Keteki sees this as a way of directly transmitting, infiltrating a whole culture into people's lives somewhere totally different. I like the idea. It's a great business idea too, though she's not very interested in that part yet.'

'Oh, you've been there,' Joy mama said. 'That's good.'

'I have,' Ved said. 'But I haven't asked her—you remember I said I wanted to ask her to marry me? I thought that was the next step when I talked to you in August. But I can't ask her to spend her life with me when she doesn't even want to spend the weekend with me.' He shrugged.

Joy mama got up to switch on the light. 'Shall we have a glass of beer, Ved?' he suggested.

'That sounds good.'

'Tell me more about your life in Uzan Bazar.' Keteki's uncle laughed and waved a hand in apology. 'It seems so unlikely that you are there. Don't take it badly, Ved. But you are our English friend. What do you do all day?'

'My days,' said Ved, accepting a glass of beer. The cold, soapy liquid was refreshing. 'Well, the lady who cleans for me comes earlier than I'd like, sort of whenever she wants. Often, she wakes me up. I make coffee and sit about waiting for her to go.' He smiled. 'I don't have a lot of furniture yet, but I'm buying some, from ads online. Nice vintage wooden furniture. That's one thing I've been doing—looking at bad photos of wooden furniture and phoning people to go and look at it, fixing up with someone to collect it for me. I've become friendly with the drivers in two of the auto stands nearby.'

Joy mama laughed and nodded. He leaned back.

Encouraged, Ved went on. 'If it's early enough, I go for a walk after Sagar ... after the cleaner has left. She's an odd person, or at least I don't seem to understand her very well. I tried to talk to her in Assamese, but I think she's Bihari. There are a lot of Biharis in the area. Near the river actually. I sometimes have tea made by a Bihari man. It's so beautiful, the river—it makes no sense that such a wild, huge river flows through the city. The mist over it in the morning is incredible. Kuwoli,' he smiled at Joy mama.

'Ah yes! You're learning Assamese.'

Ved nodded. 'One of Keteki's friends, Lueit, helped me find someone who would teach me. I go to Pinky, my teacher, in the afternoon three times a week. Her other students are six or seven years old. I don't think she quite believed that a person could be an adult and, you know, somewhat functional and intelligent but not know or be able to pick up Assamese.' He shook his head.

Joy mama poured the rest of the beer into their glasses. 'And what do you study in your lessons?'

'I found a book, in a shop in Pan Bazar,' Ved said. 'It's not great, but it's a start. Some words and vocabulary and stuff, though it's old fashioned. Then I just buy books in Assamese. I got some Amar Chitra Katha at the book fair: *Xati aaru Xibo*, one about Xonkordeb ... I got a book of prize-winning short stories, though they're a little difficult for me. And a book of proverbs, fokora jujona. I remember you telling me about them the first time I came here.' He laughed.

Joy mama smiled. 'I have to say, Ved, you are revealing hidden depths. I don't mean to be rude. I always liked you, but I didn't quite see this capacity for ... I don't know what the word is. I want to say devotion, yes.'

Moved, Ved looked down at his hand, and at the surface of the kitchen table, the scratches on its red surface. This was where the real life of the house had happened—he felt it in a flash, then it was gone.

'What about you?' he asked gently. 'How do your days pass?'

'Lately, Ved, I've been tidying,' Joy mama said. 'Ketu helps when she's around. This house, with just me in it—I don't know. Perhaps it is or should be the end of an era.'

'Do you have any idea where Tuku could have gone?' Ved asked.

Joy mama shook his head. 'Nothing firm. He'd begun to spend more time away, perhaps in Majuli. It's a magical place, Ved, you should go sometime. I think he found friends there. That's important, with the strange existence he has led, never knowing where he came from.'

'I suppose that could also give a person a certain freedom,' Ved said.

'True, although here, belonging is very important.'

'Mm,' said Ved. 'People always ask me where I'm from, and where my family is. I don't think it makes much sense to them that I'm here. But maybe they're just relieved that I'm not a Bangladeshi. Can I ask you … what is that about, what is the anxiety about people crossing the border?'

The other man considered. 'Language,' he said. 'Manners, a way of life. You know, we are a lazy people, but we have good manners. We are taught to live collectively, to think about others. It's problematic when there is a big movement of people, as there has been in the last fifty of sixty years, and that changes.' He splayed out his fingers in front of him and regarded them. 'They have to live too. It's frightening, however. For years we were a kingdom as though asleep—despite everything, assaults, the Burmese invasions. Ved, I think we'll go into the other room. I feel a little cold in here now that it's evening.'

As they carried the bottle and glasses through the dining room and passage, into the library, Joy mama said, 'We'll go and get Chinese food for dinner. There's a lovely place, run by a Chinese man from Shillong. Momos, chow, anything you like.'

The library room was warmer. Some of the shelves now had gaps, and a cardboard box lay on the floor. Ved gave Joy mama an inquiring glance. The other man made a deprecating gesture. 'What can I say.' He put on the standard lamp, which began to emit a soft light through its skin shade. 'Lovely lamp, bought by a horrible man, my elder brother,' he said. 'Unfortunate humans can produce good almost in spite of themselves, it seems sometimes.' As he spoke, he was pulling a fan heater on a long cord towards them. 'I get cold,' he said. 'Old age.'

They sat on the cane armchairs, the curtains covering the French doors for warmth.

'You talked about belonging,' Ved said.

'Yes, Ved.'

'But I still don't totally understand what makes Assam one place. I've been reading history books—Edward Gait, and a more recent one. And,' he smiled, 'in my Assamese Amar Chitra Katha, I read about Xonkordeb. The Ahoms, the Koch kingdom, the original tribes who were here before Hinduism. How does it all hold together? You say language is a big part of it, but I read in the newspaper about the Bodo Sahitya Sabha as well. If a place has always been a site of migration, when does that end? From when should things be preserved? I don't have an agenda on this. I've just wondered about these things.'

Joy mama smiled. 'They are good questions, Ved. I don't have much of an agenda either. Everything changes. The Ahoms used to rule Assam, now they are a minority and their own language and culture is hardly known. But perhaps Assam is like a family that survives as long as it doesn't ask what unites the different members. Of course, in the last few decades, everyone is asking questions. Everyone wants independence from someone. We Assamese wanted it from India, or many of us did; the Karbis, the Bodos and so forth want it from Assam now. I suppose we will see how it plays out.' He shrugged.

Ved smiled. 'You don't seem as anxious about this as many people,' he noted.

'Well,' said Keteki's uncle. Had he lost weight? As well as his shorn head, he looked slighter. 'I've seen so much in my life. Good, bad, terrible. In terms of the life of a society, I can't say what will turn out to have been the right thing. I do think there has been some loss, of culture, of customs, of our sensibility. People now, in the cities, don't know so much about our traditions. But those traditions also go along with a very restrictive life. I don't want to live in a traditional Assamese village.' He laughed.

A lizard on the wall behind him chirruped loudly. Joy mama smiled. 'You know the saying about the lizard? When it speaks, it's agreeing with the last thing that was said.'

'I don't think I've ever heard such loud house lizards,' Ved said. 'I have a few in my flat. They're very chatty. I only wish they were better at killing insects. There was a spider,' he shuddered. 'Enormous. Like this.' He made a gesture with his fist. 'I tried to chase it away, but it charged me.'

Joy mama shook with laughter. 'Poor Ved.'

'Then,' said Ved, quite enjoying himself, 'I told myself to be brave. What would Lachit Borphukan have done?'

Joy mama roared with laughter and slapped his thigh. 'Good one,' he said. 'So what did you do?'

'I bought a can of insecticide,' Ved said. 'And even as I murdered the spider with horrible chemicals, I was shaking with fear.' They both laughed.

'Truly this is a new life for you,' said Joy mama with irony.

'It actually is,' Ved said. 'I'm learning how to do things I haven't done much since I became an adult. There was college, then work. I'm cooking. I like going to the market. I like buying fish, or finding out what to do with vegetables I don't know. I saw these enormous peas—like huge pea pods, a bit flat, green and purple ...'

Joy mama smiled. 'Urohi,' he said, as though invoking a magical being. 'I love them.'

Ved nodded. 'I do too, now.' He remembered the misty winter evening when he'd left Pinky's house after tuition, and bought some of the monstrous beans, taken them home and fried them with green chilli. He considered further. 'It's all ... this, learning to live, it's new to me. I like it. I would have imagined I would be bored, but there's so much to learn.'

'I think we'll have a small whisky, Ved, before we go.' Joy mama went towards the drink cabinet. He returned with a bottle of Scotch in which a couple of inches remained.

When the amber liquid was in their glasses and they had clinked, Ved said, 'Keteki said she wanted to be bored. With me.'

Her uncle chuckled. 'Did she, Ved?'

'Yes,' said Ved. In his mind he saw Keteki in the village where she now spent most of her time, living in the bamboo house rented to her by a local farmer. It had been early in the morning, and she'd been naked, her body golden in the light filtered through the bamboo walls as she stretched to take down the mosquito net from its nails. 'I'm not sure what she meant,' he said.

'Women can be terribly inscrutable,' said Joy mama.

A little later, they were in a very old Maruti car. 'Sorry, Ved, there's no heating. This beast is ancient,' Joy mama said. 'Though, luckily, much younger than her owner.' He turned on the ignition and the car jerked. 'Oops, I left it in gear. Oh yes. Handbrake. No issues, Ved, we're getting there. Don't worry, you're not going to die. Not in this car, anyway.' The car gave a groan and a shudder. Ved couldn't help looking at Joy mama, who was wrapped up in a jacket and a scarf. 'I know, Ved,' he said. 'I look like a mad old Bengali from Calcutta. In the end, perhaps it's simply a question of choosing one's clichés ...'

The car moved slowly through the silent streets of Choladhara. Jorhat at night was spooky. The main streets were harshly lit, but whole areas were soft with darkness. To Ved, the front gardens and wooden verandas of the houses they passed seemed to resonate with spectral disappointment.

'Do you think there are a lot of ghosts in Jorhat?' he asked.

'Yes, Jorhat is very haunted,' nodded the older man, nearly stalling as he paused to let a sudden, bundled-up pedestrian pass out of the mist.

'Why?' Ved said.

'You know, Ved ... there are so many layers of history in upper Assam. Even the Lucifer factory, where you went, in Moran. My father knew the original owner, perhaps the grandfather of the man you worked with. There was some trouble locally—something about the land the factory is built on. It was tribal land originally. He worked in the tea trade, you know, and his wife went back home after a time, something like that. I think he may have had a local housekeeper who was his companion. Some gossip. This was such a long time ago. But such disputes are common. This place is full of scars. The Mataks, the Rajbongshis, then the tea tribes, who were originally brought from Bihar and the east of the mainland. They have their own language, a mix of their languages and Assamese. And their conditions of work—' He turned left onto the main road. 'Here we are. But where will I park? Ah yes.' Joy mama began to address the driver of another, larger car. 'Do go, do carry on. Good man. Now I can get in there. If I could see anything from the back. Oh dear! But we were hardly going slowly.'

They got out in front of a small shop labelled Chung Fu. Joy mama opened the door. A cloud of breath seemed to escape him, or perhaps it was starchy warmth coming from the shop? Ved followed him in.

'Chung!' said Joy mama. He shook hands with a large Chinese man in a black hoodie and explained that Ved was a friend from England, staying in Guwahati.

Chung smiled. 'You must have been to Shillong,' he said.

'No,' Ved said. 'I've been planning to.' He was waiting for Keteki, who'd promised shortly after he arrived that they'd go to Shillong together.

'That's my place,' Chung said.

'Chung makes the best chow and momos,' Joy mama said. 'What would you like? Chicken? Pork? Something spicy?'

When they were leaving, Joy mama said, 'It's good food, Ved. I am a very basic man. It's one of the reasons I've managed to be happy all my life. Could you carry this?' He handed Ved the takeaway bag and opened the car doors.

Soon after dinner, Ved was in bed in Keteki's room. He thought again of the night he'd spent with her in the village over a month ago. He'd asked what was going through her mind. 'I came here to be with you,' he said. 'In case it isn't obvious.'

In the dark, Keteki chuckled. 'Sweet of you, Ved.'

'I'm not being sweet!' he said. 'I wish you'd stop pulling that Assamese bullshit on me.'

'I thought you were in love with everything Assamese.'

'I'm in love with you. Look,' Ved began.

'Listen,' she said. 'When I was in London, spending time with you … I could feel something happening to me. I started getting jealous, thinking about other women you'd been with.' The sleepy calm of her voice was at odds with her words. Ved couldn't absorb it. 'Your first girlfriend, all the encounters you must have when you travel. It's not as though I lead a celibate life.' Ved twitched. 'But,' Keteki went on, 'I could feel myself falling down this thing …'

'Rabbit hole,' Ved said.

'Maybe,' Keteki said. 'I didn't like it, Ved. I'm not good at all that. It was like a layer of nightmare under everything. Sometimes I think that's how things are, in fact.'

'Nightmare?' Ved said. There were rustling noises outside the shadows in the bamboo hut, but to him it felt safe and warm.

'A shadow side,' Keteki said. She turned over, and her voice became smaller, more resigned. 'The ways people like to fuck. The things they do and don't tell people about. Ghosts. Fairy stories.' She sighed. 'Things that go on in the dark. Things adults do to children.' The bamboo outside rustled.

'Hang on,' Ved said. He put his arms around her. 'All this because of other women? I haven't been with anyone else since you were in London.'

'Hm,' she said.

'I didn't know how I'd feel,' Ved said. 'But it turned out I didn't want to.'

'Okay,' she said sleepily.

'I mean it,'

'Thanks, Ved.'

'Don't you feel the same?' Ved asked, his voice tight.

'I think in some ways I find it easier being alone,' Keteki said, sleepy in the darkness. 'There are always people, of course … But it's easier to keep things at a distance, better than trying to go into the nightmare and come out. It's …'

'Shh,' Ved said. 'It's going to be fine. Don't worry.'

Now, in Jorhat, in the middle of the night, Ved woke and thought, adults doing things to children? Why didn't I ask? He'd been so preoccupied with moving ahead with things that he hadn't really stopped to listen.

He thought he heard a sound in the courtyard. The curtain moved, and he remembered lying in bed with Keteki the first time he'd come here, and Tuku's voice outside. He'd grown to love this old house, at times sinister with silences, but graceful too: the doors that led into the garden, the cane furniture in the library room, the quietness of the kitchen and its containers of rice and dal, the bottle of mustard oil, the cats' food bowls. After dinner, as Ved was on his way to bed, something sharp had struck his foot: Pingala, lying on the floor behind the bookshelf and swiping at Ved as he passed. He had left the familiar, London, the BBC radio news in the morning as he drank his coffee in his kitchen, he'd left his job, and now he was here. He didn't have to worry about money, it was true—but what would he do next, if Keteki didn't want him?

He remembered their morning in the village. Ved had sat drinking tea in the sun while she went around visiting different workers. Outside their houses, women worked on small looms that they held in their laps; one woman was weaving more elaborate cloth on a larger, freestanding loom. Keteki had shown him a bag of black cotton that she'd been given in Mizoram. Ved inhaled its inky, earthy scent. 'You're part of something,' he said to Keteki.

He got up in search of a drink to help him get back to sleep. Trying to be quiet, he made it to the library and pushed open the door. A shard of cold white light came through the curtains onto a wing chair, touched the stand of the lamp with the camel skin shade. Ved remembered he would need a glass, and went to the kitchen. He left the light on, and came back to the book room. The cats had arrived. Pingala sat on the stool next to Ved's chair and watched as he poured himself a whisky. Ved turned on the standard lamp and wished he hadn't; there was probably a council of spectres in the garden, watching through the gap in the curtain. Of course, they might have helpful advice for him. But more likely they'd send him into a swamp and watch him drown. He sat in the yellow pool of lamplight and closed his eyes. At night, insomniac, it seemed imperative to put the things of the world in order. But life simply tumbled on from one incomplete, chaotic state to another. '*Nature*,' intoned a sub-Attenborough voice in Ved's head, commenting on visuals of a flooded rice field and a pond with lotuses, 'is always in *flux*. The *natural* world is never at a *stand*still. Indeed—'

A goddess, dressed in a red-and-gold mekhela, took Ved by the hand and led him from one floating island to another in the river, never pausing. All around them were fish flying up into the air and then diving back down, a kingfisher, the sun sparkling off the water, and sudden flashes of smoke and fire, wills o' the wisp. But where are we *going*? Ved wanted to ask. There was no time—he followed the inexorable, lithe-waisted goddess, his feet growing weary. He had sight of their destination: a mountain top, wreathed in mists, on which sat a figure in meditation. The man's eyes were closed, but as Ved and the goddess approached, a glowing red eye appeared in the middle of his forehead. Then the figure, modestly dressed in a flame-coloured kurta and yellow dhuti, opened his seeing eyes. It was Tuku.

On Monday night, after seven hours of travelling, Ved stepped off the train and into the station at Paltan Bazar in Guwahati. He looked forward to going home. The streets on his short walk were pitch dark and cold. It was easier to walk on the road than step onto the high, uneven pavements then down again. Near the Ideal Pharmacy, sentinel of the home stretch, he passed a homeless man and leaned down to give him some money. A sardonic nod was the response. But at the gate of Ved's apartment block, the laconic white-haired watchman greeted him. 'So you're back, dada?' It was the first homecoming since Ved had moved in.

The flat was cold and dark. He put on the living-room light, then the Lucifer in the kitchen. The wiring was old; many of the sockets would only take an incandescent. Rajen had sent Ved a big box of leftover Lucifers from Moran, old stock. 'Ved,' he had said on the phone, 'don't forget us. You and I are still friends.'

Ved put on the hot water in the bathroom and phoned Hot Pot to order crispy honey chilli chicken and noodles. He pottered around, unpacking, and hanging up his mosquito net before taking a shower. He'd spent a day scrubbing the bathroom with bleach when he moved in, but it had retained some gunk in the corners. Trying not to think about enormous spiders, he soaped himself. The shower was never quite warm enough or copious enough, but Ved wasn't paying that much rent, and didn't want to bother his landlord. He was a different Ved, indeed, than in London, where he would have phoned a plumber or got one of the office PAs to do it for him. Sometimes he thought of his London flat, the plush towels, the perfect underfloor heating. Here, everything was tendentious: wires freed themselves of their casing and in some places were sellotaped to the wall. Cupboard doors hung on one hinge; the extractor fan in the kitchen had given up, and was a gaping hole through which rain, insects and small birds entered. The last time Ved had been away for a few days, he'd returned to find a tiny sparrow sleeping on the pelmet of his bedroom window. They were flatmates for a few days more, the sparrow hurrying in at dusk to go to bed. But he roused Ved urgently every morning before 4 a.m., and Ved took to shutting the window in the evening. Still, the little invasion had been delightful. And he'd been so sure he was someone who needed his space.

He dried himself and was putting on a T-shirt and track pants when the doorbell rang. He left the towel around his neck, found his wallet, and hurried to the door.

'Hi Ved,' said Keteki, standing a little to the side of the doorway.

'Hi,' said Ved. After a moment, he removed the towel from his neck.

'Sir,' said the Hot Pot boy, arriving behind Keteki.

'I'll ... come in,' Ved said to Keteki. She smiled at him and the dazed-looking Hot Pot boy. In the last three months, he doubted the boy had ever seen Ved in any sort of company.

'The place looks great,' said Keteki, while Ved tipped the delivery boy enormously. 'I rang the bell one floor down. A young Mizo boy answered. I was a bit confused.' She laughed at herself and pulled up the oversized hoodie slipping off her shoulder. She looked great, and she was looking great in Ved's flat.

'Want to look around?' Ved put the food on the table and took her hand. 'I bought the sofa and chairs from a Bengali family who were moving back to Calcutta.'

She laughed. 'You've put up little pictures.'

One of the things Ved had framed was a clipping from the *Assam Tribune*, the day he moved into the flat: HABIT IS A GREAT DEADENER—S. Beckett.

'This is the kitchen,' he continued. 'There's a finite amount of improvement to be had in cleaning this flat, unfortunately.' He tried not to look at the walls, painted in a turquoise wash that was powdery and impermanent.

Keteki nodded. 'Guwahati is dusty. You have to repaint every few years.'

'But aren't you just covering over the dirt, then?'

'Nothing is clean, Ved. Not in this country.' Her eyes were a warm, clear brown, and her high voice was husky like frosted glass.

Ved tried to keep hold of the conversation. 'Assam?' he managed.

'India,' Keteki said.

'Right. So, this is the dining table. I got it from a suspicious-looking lady whose husband works at the medical college. I think she thought I might have an orgy on it.' Keteki looked sceptical.

'This is the study. And this is the bedroom.' The bed, bedside table and a chest of drawers on which he had baskets from the riverside marketplace.

'Bamboo baskets,' Keteki said. 'Now you're really becoming a local. We use them for keeping vegetables.' Ved kept small items in his: socks, his wallet, keys.

'Do you want some dinner?' he asked.

'Sweet of you, Ved. But I have to meet some friends. They'll pick me up soon. You go ahead, do eat.'

'Have a bite,' he said. He got out plates and cutlery, and they sat down. She smiled at the takeaway containers and the Assamese newspaper, which she picked up gingerly. '*Pratidin* is a little right wing for me,' she said. 'Can you read this?'

'The headlines,' said Ved. 'I don't understand everything.'

Keteki smiled. She took a bite of honey-glazed chicken. 'Mm, Hot Pot,' she said.

'You know,' said Ved, 'at the risk of sounding like a broken record, I do want to be with you properly. That's why I'm here, in part.'

She considered. 'What's the other part?' She wound some noodles round her fork.

'Well, this is an incredible place, and a beautiful language,' Ved said. 'I'm enjoying getting to know it. Though I don't think I ever will. I keep hearing about other foreigners who have, like that German woman who rented the flat in your aunt's house. It's annoying. I used to think I was good at languages. Yours seems to be booby-trapped against outsiders, though.'

Keteki crowed with laughter.

'You know,' Ved said. 'All the indefinite articles. A hundred and fifty different ways to say "a something"?'

'Oh yes,' she said. 'You mean like "eta" and "ekhon".'

'Ejowr juta,' offered Ved, a pair of shoes. 'Edal goss,' a tree.

Keteki frowned. 'I think ejupa goss is a little better,' she said.

'And then the proverbs.'

She smiled. 'You're learning them? Do you remember any?'

'The only one I remember is about turmeric and ginger,' Ved said.

She laughed again. 'Try it?'

'How does it go … "Adak dekhi uthil ga, keturiye bule, 'Muku kha'"? That blew my mind when Pinky explained it. The turmeric looks at the ginger and says, "Eat me too". And the gloss explains that ginger is a useful everyday item, but the turmeric is envious because it isn't. A root has a speaking part in a two-line proverb. It's so surreal.'

Keteki chuckled. 'Keturi isn't exactly turmeric,' she said. 'I think it's related, but it's different. It's supposed to be good for the complexion.'

'I know,' Ved said. 'I saw it being sold just outside, across the junction, and I thought it was ginger and tried to buy some, but when I asked for it, the man selling it mimed face-washing gestures. I thought he was insane.'

Keteki laughed again. 'We all are, here, Ved.' Her phone began to buzz. 'Ved, my friends are downstairs. I'll drop in later if you're up.' She rose to put away her plate.

'I'd love that,' Ved said.

He remained half-awake till late that night, wondering when she'd arrive. But early in the morning, he awoke to a text from her. 'Sorry Ved, it got late. Do you want to go to Shillong this weekend?'

23

Hills

'What now?' wondered Ved. The cab driver had stopped; the morning was smoky.

Another man stuck his head in the window to argue. After a while, he was given some money; they set off.

Paltan Bazar was nightmarish: dirty buildings plastered with posters and signs. After a while, they took the flyover, then were on the GS road, lined with shops and malls, that connected Guwahati and Shillong.

The driver, an elderly Bihari, complained relentlessly in Hindi. It was too cold, they weren't paying him enough, why didn't they let him pick up another fare too, he had an errand to run at Nongpoh. Ved answered from time to time in his poor Hindi. Keteki, tucked into her oversized hoodie, demurred: 'We could just have waited till the evening and driven up with my friends.' Then she gave up and slept through the journey. Ved gazed out at the dusty roads of Ri Bhoi district, and then at the hills, red chalk with scar-like quarries.

Once they arrived at the outskirts of Shillong, the car sat in traffic for an hour on the single-lane road. Ved peered into the windows of the many meat shops they passed and saw

sides of pig hanging up, he read the names on shop signs:
Kharkongor, Nongkynrih, Kurkalong, Lyngdoh. South-east-
Asian-looking men in dark jackets and trousers watched the
passing cars with narrowed eyes and spat red tobacco sputum
onto the pavement; tiny rosy-cheeked children with straight
hair and bright knitted sweaters played together near women
in checked cotton wrappers.

Finally they arrived at the guesthouse. The driver
complained vociferously about the one-way system, the
punitive attitude of Meghalaya Traffic Police and the time it
was taking Ved to wake Keteki.

Goaded, Ved snapped, 'Don't shout at me!'

Keteki roused. 'Are we here?'

The guesthouse, a wooden-framed Assam-type building,
was sweet. Keteki decided to finish her nap, and Ved, starving,
went for a walk in what he thought was the direction of town.
The last of the sunshine was bright and cast sharp shadows.
He passed women selling baskets of orange fruit and, a little
later, arrived at the main shopping street, just as the light was
fading. Suddenly it was night, clouds of exhaust fumes and
breath in the moist, cold air. People packed into shared taxis;
boys and girls strolled along the pavement, some in colourful
wraparound skirts, others in jeans and leather jackets. It took
him a little while to find his way back, and when he arrived,
Keteki was ready, sitting on the bed, mutinous because he'd
gone out and hadn't heard his phone.

'Let's get something to eat,' Ved cajoled. They went to a
new bar, five floors up in a glass hotel on the main road and
ordered burgers, and a beer for Ved, a glass of wine for Keteki.

'So,' he said, 'tell me how it's going. Work, the village?'

For a second, she held his hand, and he smiled involuntarily
at how good it felt.

'It's going well,' she said. 'We have a little stock building up. I think we're making some good pieces. You've seen some of the earlier ones, but the work is improving. Wraparound skirts, tops. I've sent pictures to a friend in London, a friend in Paris. It seems as though we might be able to find places to carry them. I think we should do a website, but I haven't yet found the right person.' She paused to take a bite of her fish burger. Ved watched a group of girls, maybe in their late teens, in leather jackets and short skirts or tight jeans. One of them was showing off long, apparently freshly painted fingernails to the others, who were laughing and admiring them. She stopped and gave Ved a direct look.

'There's a lot ahead,' Keteki went on. 'If it grows, I'll need to start thinking about permissions, the different taxes we have to pay, an export licence. To begin with, I just want to get going with production and get people used to this being a part of their lives. But the admin could easily—' She broke off and followed Ved's gaze. 'Are you listening?'

'The admin?' invited Ved.

Keteki ate a couple more bites of her burger in silence and drained her wine. 'Why,' she said suddenly, 'would you come here for the weekend with me, ask me how my life is and then zone out to stare at some girls?'

'Oh come on,' Ved said. 'You slept the entire way here.'

'I didn't realise there were rules about when I could *sleep*.'

'Why are you angry? Look, I've been trying to see you since I got here. I—'

'Well, now you know,' Keteki said, 'what it feels like. How do you think it was for me in London?'

'What?'

'Well, you going on endlessly about your ex-girlfriend or whatever. And who else were you sleeping with? I—'

'No, no, no,' Ved said. 'I wasn't. I just didn't know where this … where we … but then I realised—'

The waiter appeared. 'Sir, can I repeat your drinks?'

He had to repeat himself.

'I,' Ved began.

'We should go, Jimmy's downstairs,' Keteki said, looking at her phone.

Ved had a vision of the evening, Keteki amid a clutch of her male friends, as usual, Ved possibly left behind at some point, or in any case introduced as her friend, standing politely by. Why do it to himself?

'I'll have a beer,' he told the waiter, and to Keteki, he said, 'You know, I think I'll skip it. I'll be at the hotel.'

Just before she turned away, the expression on her face— was it anger? Or surprise?—registered on him, but he shrugged it off.

24

Gold Spot

'I DO REMEMBER,' Keteki said. 'Oh, they've sort of melted.' She tried to unpeel one of the rubber Gold Spot Jungle Book tokens from a pile. Was that Mowgli? 'I think you could send them off and claim something. How on earth did we get so many?'

'The head waiter at the Gymkhana was a great friend of yours, remember?' said Joy mama. 'He saved them for you when he could.'

Keteki dropped the rubbery mass back into the carton. 'Let it go,' she said. 'All of it. I don't even know the people it used to belong to any more.'

Her uncle smiled. 'Isn't much of this yours?'

'That's what I mean,' she said.

'I feel the same,' he said, touching her shoulder. 'Why are we keeping all this? Not for me. But of course, there may be further generations of this family to come.'

'Throw it away,' Keteki said. 'There are memories I'd be glad to see go.'

'I know, Ketu.'

'I still can't sleep in that room,' she said. 'But other things of his don't bother me, that awful skin lampshade, for instance. From which the light is so lovely.' She looked at her good uncle. 'What happened almost feels like a ghost story that used to be terrifying when I was a child. Not quite, but as though it had happened to someone else. In the ashram, I wasn't thinking about it directly, but I cried a lot for the first week or two. I couldn't stop.'

'Ketu,' said Joy mama.

She held his hand. 'I'm not trying to make you feel bad. For a long time it was there inside me. I think it made me feel I could never be close to anyone.'

They left the store room and continued the tour of the house. He said, 'He knows he can never come back here. What a strange life it must be for him.'

Keteki smiled.

'I know, I know,' said Joy mama. 'I've cut myself off from things too, but it's different. I hear from people, they telephone, even if I no longer attend weddings and all that sort of thing.' As he spoke he was putting things from the corridor shelves into a plastic sack. Keteki put out her hand to carry it. 'Sweet of you, Ketu. You were always such a companionable child.' He put his large warm hand on her head for a moment. 'We are the survivors,' he said. 'The renegades. And now, the study.' They went into the book room.

Keteki rolled herself a cigarette, aware of her uncle watching her. 'If you're wondering, yes, it does feel pretentious to do this in front of you,' she said.

He smiled. 'Give me a puff.' Afterwards, he grimaced. 'That first little lift is nice. But now I feel sick. I don't think I'll do that again.'

'You never tried it when you were younger?'

He nodded. 'Oh yes. It was the same then.'

They both laughed.

'I don't like the idea of dependence,' Keteki said. 'Habit. Speaking of which, if I get married, will you come? A little thing, not a big thing.'

'Oho!' Her uncle smiled. 'I like Ved. He isn't stupid. So he finally asked?'

'No,' Keteki said. 'I'll probably have to ask him, if I can stop changing my mind about it every ten minutes. I'm afraid of his faults,' she confessed. 'And then when I think harder, I'm terrified of mine.'

'It's not surprising,' said her uncle, 'when you consider the first people you loved, those who were meant to look after you. I know she's my sister. But she was a terrible mother. Consistency is a great virtue in a parent.' He roamed, looking at the bookshelves. 'I don't think I have the energy for the books just now, Ketu. It's such a trap, with this absurd upbringing of ours. Either one wants to hang on to all of them or they may as well all go. Some must have their value. The Assamese novels, the periodicals, the Puja numbers. Yet, in a way, they too are so much dead skin, aren't they?'

'Are you planning to take vanvas and go to the forest?' Keteki demanded. Then she laughed at herself. 'I shouldn't be possessive. About people. You, Ved. I have the urge to know, to control things, but the more I give in to it, the more anxious I become.' She was leaning against the back of the wing chair, and absent-mindedly turned on the standard lamp with its skin shade. A warm, soft light filled half the room.

Her uncle smiled. 'Why do you need to project into the future? If you want to be with Ved now, that's enough.'

'I'm nervous,' she said. 'About tying my happiness to someone else's vagaries.'

'But haven't you already done so? Isn't it done, rather? You are living a human life, after all. That's what you chose.' He sat down on the worn Kashmiri rug, cross-legged. Keteki looked at him. His eyes behind the spectacles were dark and open. 'Life can be as vast as the sky,' he said, 'and change all the time. Let yourself be inconsistent. You always know what to do.'

They were both still.

'Let's get some dinner,' he said. 'Tidying can resume tomorrow. You're here for a few days, aren't you?'

When they were getting ready to go to the car, he sighed. 'I do miss Tuku, you know. That boy was such good company for me. But it's all right. Life has its phases.'

25

The fire starter

'VED, GREAT TO see you. Are you frozen again?'

Ved smiled at Rajen. 'It's not warm on the train. But I'm more suitably dressed this time.' He gestured at his jacket, sweater and scarf.

'You look good. You've gone a bit native,' Rajen said with a twinkle. 'Come, come, the car's just here.' As they walked, he put a hand on Ved's shoulder. 'You know, we tend to prefer the bus over the train. But it's all the same. Have you eaten?' He laughed. 'Look at me, I'm talking as though I were your mother. But you are the guest, after all.' When they were in the car, he continued, 'It's great to see you again, Ved. And I also invited you to visit because there's something I wanted to show you, not now, but when we get to the plant.'

'Really?' Ved said. He smiled at the big man. 'You're back in production?'

'Oh yes, yes.' Rajen let in the clutch, and they left the station area. 'CFLs, tube lights, but also LEDs. We have a new range of fancy LEDs. They look like filament bulbs, very pretty. A couple of the new restaurants in Guwahati have fitted them.'

'Almost like real light,' Ved said.

Rajen laughed. 'Good one, Ved.'

They were driving through town. 'I have a friend here,' Ved said. 'A friend's uncle. I've been here a few times now.'

'Jorhat,' Rajen said. 'Wonderful place. So much history. The court used to be here, after it was in Sibsagar. And the Sahitya Sabha is here.'

'How are things at the factory?' Ved asked.

'Well, something unexpected happened. But things have been fine, things are ... You know, politically a lot has been going on. I don't suppose you remember the little temple we had in the compound?'

'Phiringoti Devi?' Ved asked.

Rajen jerked his head round to look at Ved. 'Wonderful fellow, Ved. So observant!'

Ved began to beam, before realising he was being oiled up, as the Assamese expression has it.

'The oddest thing happened with the murti,' Rajen went on. 'The statue. One morning we were opening up, and she'd disappeared.'

'What?'

Rajen nodded vigorously. 'Amazing. Of course, someone must have removed her. But everything came to a halt. It was around the time we stopped making the Lucifers. We had no idea what to do. The workers were very unhappy.'

'Who do you think took the statue?'

'Oddest *thing*, Ved. They said she left, walked off.' The big man widened his eyes. A moment later, he looked at the road, where a small, pretty cow was sitting in the middle of the lane. Rajen yanked the steering wheel. 'Sorry, Ved.'

'So the statue was never found?' Ved asked.

'Never found,' Rajen said. 'But something else happened. We talked with the workers, listened to them, met some of their demands. An association for the factory, a table tennis room, better facilities for their meals, a bus, that sort of thing. I was torn, I admit it. What they were asking for wasn't unreasonable, but you have to be careful. If people sense weakness ...'

Ved sighed, thinking of Keteki.

'But anyway, work resumed, we modified the factory line, went back to making the usual bulbs. Business is fine. No trouble, no excitement. I wonder, myself, about moving on in a little while. I don't know.'

'But the statue?'

'We put in a new one, Ved. Made the temple a bit bigger, a pukka building, cement. We put fresh flowers for her every morning and evening. It was one of the demands. Many of the workers are xonkori, but all of us felt the temple was lucky for us. It's difficult to explain. And the other thing—I'd wanted to wait till we got to the factory. But we found out how the fire started.'

'What was it?' They passed the colourful painted bamboo walls of the restaurant where they'd stopped the first time Rajen took Ved to Moran.

'I don't know if you remember one of the workers. Hajong lady—you may recall her dress? It's the traditional one, a sort of red-striped wrap. Very pretty.'

'I think so,' Ved said. He saw the woman's grave face, her bright clothing.

'We realised when we opened again. She works on boxing and checking the bulbs before they are packed. There is a lot of flammable material around her—card, that sort of thing.'

'But she seemed so quiet,' Ved said wonderingly. 'Why would she do it?'

Rajen laughed. 'Yes,' he said. 'It wasn't deliberate. The oddest thing I've seen. Her skin is very dry, it seems. Working near the rubber conveyor belt caused static. Sparks off her body. One of them caught some dry packaging and made it smoke. That was at the end of the day shift, and when we closed before a holiday, the card was smouldering. It was enough.' He raised an eyebrow.

'You can't be serious?'

Rajen nodded. 'Strangest thing, but then strange things do happen. Consider all the things that meant the fire broke out. Normally there is a night shift, and the smouldering cardboard would have been stamped out.'

'Sparks off her *skin*,' said Ved.

Rajen slowed, then drove around some cows sitting in the middle of the road. 'Women,' he said with gusto. 'Extraordinary beings. I'm surprised more of them don't cause factory fires.'

The next morning, Ved texted Keteki photographs of the new temple, with red hibiscus strung over the door, and of the goddess, a plaster idol oddly devoid of mystery, with black hair, almond-shaped eyes and red lips.

'It's funny,' he told Rajen over a hungover cup of coffee at the big man's office before he set off. 'It sort of feels almost as if the idol is still missing.'

Rajen looked at his hands. 'Well, Ved,' he said. 'Of course. I mean, the idol is—what's that phrase? The object of our affection. Not the affection itself. God doesn't live in a statue, Goddess still less so. But we keep the statue to show …'

'Observance,' suggested Ved.

'These are for you, Ved. The new Lucifer, if you like.' Rajen pushed a box of four bulbs across the desk. They were marked Philoment Vintage Style Bulb. 'Observance,' he said, and twiddled one end of his moustache. 'Maybe just love?'

26

Full moon

'I DON'T REALLY have the time for this,' Keteki said.

Ved looked at her. Her face was illuminated by the winter sun. She pulled her jacket around her, and sat cross-legged, self-contained. He softened and took her hand, and she smiled at him.

The wind ruffled what looked like a large lake, or an ocean. It was the river. Its currents went in different directions; islands of water plants floated by. The sky was open and pale, and there was a wind. Below them, the covered area of the ferry was crowded and noisy. Here on the roof it was pleasant. A loose knot of men sat playing cards near the chimney pipe, enjoying its warmth. Keteki had withdrawn her hand from Ved's. He folded his arms around his legs, and watched the card players and looked at her.

She had closed her eyelids; in the sun, her face grew rosy. After a time, she opened her eyes. 'Winter sun is tiring,' she murmured. 'You want to sit in it and get warm, but it drains you.' She rubbed her face and twisted round, one hand on her knee. 'Ah. We're nearly there.'

All the passengers were getting ready to disembark. Those on the roof waited, and as the others poured out from under the covered deck, the roof dwellers began to jump down. Ved offered Keteki a hand. So this was Majuli, he thought, as his foot touched the soil. An island in the river that was the blood of Assam. Maybe Majuli was the quintessence of the place, a heart.

Keteki explained to the young taxi driver where they wanted to go. She and Ved sat in the back of the Maruti van, its windows open. He held her hand and looked onto green paddy fields, brown and white xaalikas, the sound of bells and singing, and children in uniform returning from school, their faces alive. Older men in dhuti and gamusa walked on the road, straight-backed and gentle in their bearing.

There was some discussion between Keteki and the driver. He was saying he thought he might not be able to go all the way to Horen da's place—that was the owner of the cottages where they would stay. The van arrived at a small crossroads, where a few men sat near a bus stop and a cement Shiva temple, drinking tea. The driver leaned out to talk to them. Keteki also put her head out of the window. She said a few words, and a ripple of laughter went through the men.

'What did you say?' Ved asked when the driver restarted the engine. They began going down a small lane next to the flooded field.

'Our friend here was worried that the vehicle would be too heavy for the bridge. It's a light bridge, mainly for crossing on foot.'

'What did you tell him?'

Keteki smiled. 'I told him we are not heavy people, that we are easy and light.'

'I hope that's true,' Ved said. She looked at him, light as a pinprick, opened her mouth as if to speak, then glanced away.

The van trundled over the fragile bridge, the bamboo creaking; a motorbike passed in the other direction and the driver tutted. But they got to the village, and drove through it, more bamboo huts, older trees, to reach the gate of the cottages.

'Well,' said Keteki, as they returned to the little veranda of their bamboo cottage after dinner. 'Hm, I don't think we can sit here.' She popped into the room and turned out the outdoor light just as Ved removed one insect from his eye, another from his mouth. 'Dessert,' he said. 'I guess.'

'Actually some insects are considered a delicacy,' Keteki noted. 'For example, silk worms, boiled in the cocoon then fried.' She sat down on the steps.

'Have you tried them?'

'Ugh, no, I couldn't. But they're meant to be delicious.'

Ved laughed. Large beetles periodically crashed into his face. He leaned against the railing of the balcony and looked down at her. 'Where are your rollies?' he asked.

'I stopped,' Keteki said. 'They made me feel sick. Sometimes the thought of them was lovely. But I think I've realised that the less I do to my body, or myself, the happier I am.' She chuckled. 'I've been growing some nice leg hair. I didn't have time to go and get waxed. The women I work with tell me to do something about myself. But I've just been so happy.' She leaned against the railing too, and Ved stroked her head for a moment.

'Look at the moon,' Keteki said. 'There are all these superstitions about not going out at night when there's a full moon. Ghosts. Things come and get you.'

'Good idea, let's go in.'

'No. I may wish to give my soul to the moon.'

'Okay.'

'Look at it,' Keteki said. The moon was huge, pale gold, incredibly bright. Keteki sat gazing upwards, as though receiving a transmission.

'I'm really glad to hear that you're happy,' Ved said eventually. 'Can you tell me more about it?'

'Let's walk,' Keteki said. She was up and off already.

'Now? In the dark?' He followed her.

'Haven't you seen the moon?'

'But it's the countryside. There's no other light at all.'

'What worries you more, Ved? Ghosts? Or tripping and twisting your ankle?'

They let themselves out of the gate, and closed it behind them, then turned to walk up the mud lane that led to a crossing. 'I think the river is this way,' Keteki said. 'You think we're having a private night-time moment,' she went on. 'But you don't know what a village is like. Tomorrow, everyone we meet will know that we're the crazy foreigners who went out in the middle of a full-moon night.'

'You're not a foreigner.'

'I am here.'

'Do you mind that, the scrutiny of people? In the village where you are?' Ved had forgotten the name.

'I did at first,' Keteki said. She was ahead of him but stopped, to his surprise and delight, to take his hand. 'For a while I tried to fit in, sit back, understand how things worked.'

'That's what I'd do,' Ved said.

'But it wasn't me,' Keteki said. 'And then I figured out how to make things work, how to achieve ... I wouldn't say efficiency, but something.'

'What did you do?'

'I just started asking people to do things for me. Errands. Showing them how I preferred things to be done, where to keep things, how we would organise our materials, all that sort of thing. I created an environment that was comfortable. They liked it.'

'Okay,' Ved said. He could only half listen. Keteki was holding his hand. Hers was warm and dry. She became alert. 'Ved,' she said.

'Yes?'

Her hand tightened. He squeezed back.

'I want to be close to you. Then something always happens.'

He stopped. They were about halfway along the path raised above a rice field. It seemed as though they might arrive at the river by continuing till a tall hedge of trees, then turning either right or left.

'You can just be an idiot at times,' Keteki continued.

Ved sighed. He looked down at her hand in the moonlight.

'You can,' she said.

'But how do you deal with the people you work with?' Ved asked. 'Now that things are going better?'

Keteki let go of his hand and put hers in her pockets. She began to walk again. 'I let them be the way they are,' she said. 'I don't expect that much. But I'm teaching them what I like. They can be lazy, they can be ineffective. And it's taking time for them to trust me. But they're starting to experience that things work better when they do things that I ask, because I'm not in this for myself. When things go wrong, it's because one person has a crisis or doesn't feel like doing things for everyone when they could just work for themselves. It's like one leaf on a tree thinking it has an independent existence.

I guess we're all liable to be like that at times.' She paused. 'I don't know which way it is. Let's try this way.' She headed right. Ved went along.

'People love to do things to please you,' he said. 'It's good you're starting to let them.'

'Oh really?'

'Yes, even me. What do you think I'm doing here?'

'I don't know. A time out? An adventure? We aren't really your business, are we?'

'You and me?'

'Us, here, in Assam.'

Ved followed her. In the shade of the trees, it was much darker. Keteki's figure, a little ahead, was nebulous, a contingent presence, not a physical object.

They came to the end of the hedge. A little ahead was the river, and a grassy bank brilliant under the full moon. Keteki turned back to him before moving on to this bright stage. 'You know, Ved, most of the happiness in my life has come from inside. Not from other people. Often, it's been despite other people.' She walked on to the bank, first sand, then grass, and sat down. Ved sat next to her. The river was louder in the dark; it rushed and sucked. The moon shone down, cool, posthumous. Ved had the urge to fight his corner, but also a sense that nothing he did this night would count. 'What would make it possible for you to be with me?' he asked.

Keteki exhaled. 'The belief that I wouldn't be angry with myself in the long run,' she said.

Ved looked at the moonlit water, softly flowing. Currents everywhere agitated the surface, an island of greenery floated past—something—an alligator? Probably a log. 'I don't know if I'd think of it that way,' he managed.

'Maybe, but what matters to me is how I think about it,' Keteki said.

Ved waited. He prayed. Something came. 'What if that's a mistake?' he said. 'Isn't it about a shared sense of things? And while we're on the subject of my sometimes being an idiot ...'

Keteki turned to him.

'I think it might be more helpful to think of me as generally an idiot,' Ved said.

She laughed. 'That's good, but you don't believe it.'

Ved tried to do his best with words. Sincerity, despite its reputation, wasn't helping. 'I do, in a way,' he said. 'From your point of view, and not only yours, I often have been an idiot. Intermittently, but quite a lot. I'm sorry. I'll try to do better.' He looked Keteki in the face, as far as possible. She sat with her back to the moon, so that her face was visible only as gleams of light and areas of obscurity.

'I'll probably fuck up repeatedly. I mean, I will. I'll piss you off. I won't betray you though. If that matters.'

'Apropos that, Ved,' said Keteki quietly, 'and thank you for the declaration. Is there anything you want to tell me about the last few months? Your life in Guwahati? Anything with anyone I know?'

'What?' said Ved.

'Tara.'

'Who?'

'Come on, Ved. Tara. The woman who always wears hotpants. She showed me some of the messages you'd sent her.'

'Oh shit. That was just flirting. I had no serious intention there at all. She invited me to drop in any time and then I said the same thing, but she only came over once, and nothing really happened. She asked to look round the flat, and then suddenly stood very close to me and said I must get lonely since you were never around.'

Keteki shrugged. 'Well, subtlety doesn't always pay.'

'I was lonely,' Ved said. 'But I got defensive and told her I like spending time on my own. Maybe that's becoming true. She got on my nerves a bit. She said it was *so sweet* that I was waiting for you, but she didn't think you were home alone thinking about me, if I knew what she meant.'

'Wow,' said Keteki.

'Well—are you saying you haven't slept with anyone else since you've known me? Or even since I've been here?'

'Oh no, I'm not saying that,' Keteki said.

Ved fell back on his elbows. 'What are we doing right now?' he asked.

Keteki hugged her knees. 'I suppose we came here partly to look for Tuku,' she said. 'Though I can't imagine we'll find him, if he doesn't want to be found. Things change. People. It's unimaginable, but that's how it is. And I think we came here to see if we—you and I—can do this. Be together.' She touched the cuff of his sweater sleeve and held his wrist. He took her hand.

'Yes,' he said. 'We can. I think it would help if you took it at face value that I want this. I'm not perfect, but I don't want anyone else. I do want you. You might have to—'

'To what?'

'Train me to do things the way you like. What is it you need from me?'

'Loyalty,' she said at once.

'Look, with Tara, that was ...'

'I know why she chased you. She loves attention, and for

some reason she's always been competitive with me. But why did you do it?'

Ved thought about it. 'Laziness, stupidity,' he said. 'And I thought you weren't thinking of me as a boyfriend. I guess I wanted to maintain some independence. But nothing happened.' He laughed. 'When I asked about her boyfriend, she explained that most of Guwahati is sleeping with someone, just not their own partner.'

Keteki chuckled. 'That's not bad. And not untrue.' She sighed. 'I can understand it, Ved. But I don't like it. It's annoying, and unsettling.'

'Maybe that's a good thing,' Ved said. 'I don't like the men you've been sleeping with.'

'Friends, Ved.'

'Whatever. I'm not offering to beat them up. But I might have to give them hard stares.'

She laughed. 'Do that.'

He leaned over to kiss her. She kissed him back, but at the same time slapped his cheek.

'That's probably fair,' Ved said.

'We're not a perfect fit or whatever,' Keteki murmured. She drew back a little. 'I don't want to be spanking you. I'm not going to be your mother or whatever creepy corporate wife fantasy you have.'

'Great,' Ved said. 'Maybe I've grown out of that anyway.'

'And what about you?' she said. 'What are you going to do with your life? Just when I find a sense of purpose you go all … floppy. Is this your plan, flaking around and pretending to learn Assamese? And how is that going, by the way?' Her laugh was throaty.

'O, soli aase, baideo,' said Ved.

Keteki laughed. 'That was almost convincing. I'm not sure you can carry on calling me baideo though.'

Ved perked up. 'No?' he said.

She laughed, then sighed. 'No,' she said. 'Come with me.'

A few hours later, elsewhere on the island, in a room also made of bamboo, a man in a red T-shirt sat quietly, cross-legged. The remains of the cooking fire still smouldered. It wasn't yet light, but he was in meditation in the hour and a half before dawn. Through him ran a current of pure life, joyous as the first iteration of a river, in the mountains after it springs from the earth. Beside him, attached to a bare fitting at the end of a single wire, burned a light bulb. As he meditated, the sparks danced.

Acknowledgements

I'D LIKE TO THANK: Pratyush Chandan Barua, Rajashri Rajkhowa Barua, and Priyanuj Barua, with particular love and thanks to the late, great Bimal Rajkhowa (Aita) for helping me read in Assamese, and Dimpi Deka for starting me off with patience and kindness; Tripi Ralte; Lueit Parasar Hazarika, Neha Parasar Kaul, and Nirvana Hazarika for all the good times; and Bela, Ravi, and Aditya Awasthi for taking care of me; special thanks to Dr Aroon Das, the late Dr Anny Das, and Burman Da; Adim Phukan, who said, 'When you put me in your book make sure you don't change my name'; Lalnunsanga Ralte; Moji Riba; Nicholas Kharkongor; and Charlee Mathlena; Veda Aggarwal, for driving and accompanying me on many research missions, and Jimmy Kelly, for being himself. Special thanks to Tim Pears, a wonderful writer and a kind friend, who read two drafts of the book, and to another writer friend, Saloni Meghani, for making time to read a draft. Thanks to Eliot Forster for the inside info on gentlemen's suiting.

I could not be more grateful to my wonderful agent Judith Murray, Alisa Ahmed, Sally Oliver, and all at Greene and Heaton; and to V K Karthika, G S Ajitha, Arunima Mazumdar, Saurabh Garge, and all at Context in India; Molly

Slight, Laura Ali, and Adam Howard at Scribe in Britain. Many thanks to Kishan Rajani for the cover.

The quotation on p.64 is from *Assam and the Assamese Mind*, by Nagen Saikia, published by the Asam Sahitya Sabha, Jorhat, 1980. I have also quoted from *Kalojia Asomiya Fokora Jujona, Dakor Boson aaru Haanthoror Haansito*, compiled by Abharani Chakrabarty, published by Sabita Prakash, Guwahati, 2014.